Fashioning A Star

A SAPPHIC ROMANTIC COMEDY

ABIGAIL TAYLOR

Prologue – Mystique/Jade

PRESENT DAY

I stared at the envelope addressed to Mystique Miller, and I cringed. As I ripped it open, I saw an invitation that read:

Reunited, and It Feels so Good

Please join us for our 15-year high school reunion on Friday, August 11th, at 5:30 p.m.

RSVP to the alumni chair by August 1st.

I couldn't believe they were sending these out so early. I guess they wanted a better turnout than the ten-year. Not that I went, but I heard through the grapevine that less than fifty people showed up out of a class of four hundred.

Oh well. I sifted through the rest of my mail and tossed the invitation along with the other junk into the recycling.

The last thing I wanted to do was subject myself to the hell I endured when I was a teenager. I might have changed a lot since then, but those scars would remain, and there was no need to open them up again.

I pushed down those negative thoughts before they took over and got ready for my day. Being a seamstress wasn't the job I had planned growing up, but it suited me. I could create works of art through multiple facets, which was what I wanted to do with my clothing line. However, that couldn't happen for a while, so I had to settle for working for others.

As I gathered my supplies for the day, my office phone rang, catching me off guard. Most of my clients called my cell.

"Hello, this is Jade," I answered skeptically, prepared for it to be a telemarketer.

"Hi, Ms. Miller?"

"Yes?" I didn't know why I said it was a question.

"This is Theo Dunbar. I am the assistant to Senator Banks, and he requests your services for his upcoming event."

That was fine and dandy, but I was booked solid. "I'm honored, but I don't have any openings right now. Please offer my apologies."

He chuckled into the phone. "I'm sorry, I shouldn't have said 'requests.' He demanded I get the best to make his suit, and that's apparently you, according to *City Magazine*."

Flattery probably worked for most people, but not me. I didn't need someone to toot my horn. However, Senator Banks reminded me of every popular kid I'd ever met—an entitled bully—which triggered all those old memories I was trying to suppress.

I lost all my bravado as I slipped into the past. The last thing I remembered was saying yes, but I wasn't even sure to what.

CHAPTER 1

Mystique / Jade

HIGH SCHOOL

"Excuse you," Tara laughed as she knocked my books out of my hand.

I had been rushing to get to my next class on the third floor. Now I would be tardy and probably get detention. I sighed as I went to pick up my stuff.

"Did you need some help?" Tara looked around, and all the other cheerleaders were there, watching, including the pack leader—Monica, who stood there like the goddess everyone, including myself, thought she was, but none of them said a word.

Even though Tara wasn't in charge, she was the loudest and did all of Monica's dirty work. Tara bent down, pretending to help, but instead, she grabbed my sketch pad and waved it in the air. That was the last thing I wanted her to see. Drawing was how I escaped this hell known as high school. Whoever said these were the "glory days" never had to deal with constant ridicule.

I was a non-conformist, so it made me an easy target for people like Monica and her gang to pick on. Not to mention my mom thought giving me a "unique" name made me special. Mystique wasn't what I would've chosen for myself, and most people thought it was funny to call me "Mistake" instead. There were so many things people could pick on me for, but it would get much worse if Tara showed everyone who my muse was.

As I lunged for my drawings, Tara held them higher. "What do you have hidden in here?" She taunted, but Damon, the star quarterback and Monica's boyfriend, came up behind her and ripped the book out of her hands before she could open it.

"Here." He handed me the pad back. Then he turned to Tara, "Why don't you fuck off? Look at her. She's scared shitless. Leave her be." He wrapped his arms around Monica and planted a kiss on her lips, which seemed to signify that the show was over.

Everyone scattered while I collected my things. "Thank you," I called out to Damon as I ran to physics. I didn't have time to wait for his response because I only had a minute to get up three flights of stairs.

Mr. Watson was a stickler for the rules, and handing out detention was like a Christmas present to himself. As I was on the final stair, I heard the bell go off, and there was no way I would get out of this. I rushed through the door to grab my seat, but he already had a slip in his hand.

"Ms. Miller, this is your third tardy, which means a week's detention." He had a bright smile as if that had made his day.

I closed my eyes tight and tried to fight back the tears. I had to work at the grocery store after school, and if I wasn't on time, I could lose my job.

"Sir—"

"No excuses. Late is late. And if it happens again, I will seek suspension."

I sighed. I couldn't risk being suspended. I needed a perfect transcript so I could get into a good college. Maybe if I took a different way to class, I could avoid all the drama and save myself some embarrassment.

When the lecture ended, I went up to Mr. Watson. "Um, sir. I'm not trying to make excuses, but I have an after-school job, and I was wondering if I could do lunch detention instead?"

4

He lowered his glasses and stared at me over the frames. "No."

He offered no further explanation. Just a flat-out no, and that was the end of the discussion—for him. But I was on the debate team, so I couldn't let it drop.

"What if I did an hour before school and also lunch detention? That way, I can make it to work on time, and it's a longer punishment.

"Ms. Miller, do you think the rules don't apply to you because you have a job? You did the crime, and you'll do the time."

That made zero sense. I'd already brokered a deal that was a harsher punishment. He was being a dick for the sake of it. But I knew this was a losing battle, and if I didn't hurry, I'd be late for my next class.

"Thank you, anyway." I ran out of the room.

Luckily, I only had to go two doors to get to Spanish. This was my favorite class because Mrs. Dorian was easygoing, and I could stare unabashedly at *her*. Sitting diagonally from me was Monica. She may have been the devil in disguise, but I couldn't help but want to take a bite of her apple.

With her straight, almost-black hair, she was like an Egyptian Goddess. Her snow-white skin was flawless, and her red, pouty lips looked delicious. I didn't even register as someone worth knowing, but this class offered me unfettered access to study her features and draw her perfectly.

As I was working on the shading of her skirt, I heard Mrs. Dorian call on me, but I had no idea what the question was.

"What?"

"En Espanol, por favor?"

At least she wasn't a prick like Mr. Watson was, so I wasn't afraid of pissing her off.

"¿Podría repetir, por favor?" The only thing I could do was ask her to repeat the question and hopefully know the answer.

"¿Conjugarás el verbo irregular saber?"

Shit. I should have been paying closer attention. Conjugating the irregular verbs wasn't as easy, but I was confident I could muddle through this one. I'd only stumbled on nosotros, but she seemed pleased.

"Muy buena. Gracias, Mysterio."

I kept my face neutral as she called out my name in Spanish. As if Mystique wasn't bad enough, but to be the same name as a comic book villain seemed worse. Then again, most people probably didn't read comics like I did, so maybe they didn't notice.

Regardless, my face was getting hotter, so I brought my attention back to my masterpiece. When I looked up from my drawing, Monica was staring at me. Oh my God. Did she know what I was doing? I couldn't risk any more embarrassment, so I closed my book and focused on class.

As soon as the bell rang, I loaded my stuff to head to detention. But before I could leave, Tara showed up. I tried dodging her, but she made it impossible.

"Where are you rushing off to, Mistake?" She grabbed my arm to keep me from leaving.

"I have detention, thanks to you. So please let me go?" I knew I sounded weak, but I had no strength left.

Tara always wanted a fight, but I just wanted to be left alone. Ignoring her didn't work, and sticking up for myself only made it worse. It was a lose-lose situation, and everything I did only seemed to add fuel to the fire.

I glanced at Monica, but I wasn't sure why. She was the ice queen, and I knew she would continue standing like a statue. Speaking to me was beneath her, and she didn't feel the need to protect me.

"Detention? That's too bad. Who's going to bag my groceries now?" She yanked my backpack and broke the strap, but luckily I had it zipped up. "Oops. I guess you'll have to get a new one, but you probably can't afford it." She cackled, and two more minions appeared as if it were a bat call.

I took some cleansing breaths and pulled out of Tara's grasp, only to have Kara and Ashleigh block my way. While trying to fight the burning feeling behind my eyes, I found the courage to push through them.

Their laughter echoed in the hall as I raced to Mr. Watson's room. When I got there, Damon was the only person there.

"Where's Mr. Watson?" I questioned as I sat down.

He tilted his head and studied me, which made me feel uneasy. I wondered if he knew how much of a crush I had on his girlfriend. It made me feel bad to covet someone who could never be mine. Especially when she belonged to Damon, and he was the only one who defended me against the mean girls.

"He said he had to jet. His dogsitter called, and something was wrong with Mr. Pookie." Damon laughed, and it was loud but soothing. "Anyway, we're free to go once the final bell rings."

"Oh. Okay. So, you had detention, too?" I didn't think jocks got in trouble.

"Sort of."

Before I could ask what that meant, the unmistakable scent of cinnamon and apples wafted through the air, drawing my attention away from him. When I glanced at the door, Monica was leaning against the frame.

"You ready?" She wrapped her hair around her finger, appearing annoyed.

Then she tilted her head just enough to make eye contact with me but never smiled or said anything. Her icy stare froze me to my core, but I didn't want to look away from those sapphire orbs. They were so dark you almost couldn't tell they were blue but appeared softer and brighter when the light hit them.

"You need a ride?" Damon called out, and I turned around to see if anyone else had walked through the back door, but it was only me. I heard that deep throaty laugh again, and he said, "I'm talking to you, Misty."

Misty? No one called me that. However, it was better than Mistake. I wasn't sure what to say, but it didn't matter because he didn't allow me to respond. He wrapped me in a one-armed hug and pulled me along as he laced his other hand with Monica's.

"Let's get out of here. Where do you need to go?" He questioned, and I still couldn't figure out what was happening.

It was like I was the top bun in a Damon sandwich, and the entire moment felt surreal. And being by his side offered me protection from the bullies, so I got over the awkwardness of it all.

When we made it to his pickup, the three of us crammed inside, and Monica was in the middle. There wasn't much room, but I didn't mind. This was the closest I'd ever been to her, and my heart was pounding like a drum. When her thigh rubbed against mine, my body felt hot and cold at the same time, and I tried to keep my emotions from spilling out.

"Are you okay?" I asked, hoping she didn't notice what her touch was doing to me.

"I'm good." She didn't elaborate but rested her arm behind my head, and I thought I might die.

This was single-handedly the worst and best day of my life. But regardless of how good I was feeling now, I knew tomorrow would be a new day of hell. And I couldn't wait to get out of this place.

CHAPTER 2

Monica

PRESENT DAY

"**W**hat do I need to do?" I held up the wrap-around dress, but I was skeptical it would stay in place if I moved too much. "I don't want another fiasco like the last time when my top popped open and hello—Ms. Titty made her debut appearance."

My stylist didn't seem overly concerned with my wardrobe malfunction, but I was in the public eye and couldn't be flashing people without it ending up on Page Six. Not that I was famous, but being on television made my life much more publicized, even if I was only a news anchor. People felt entitled to know about me, and when I slipped up, they were more than happy to share it with the world.

"It's not going anywhere. And you can wear a bra this time, so if it does, at least no one will see your nipple."

I stared at her as if she'd lost her mind. "Stacy! I don't care if there's nipple or not. I don't want to show everyone my boobs. If I did, I would have become an exotic dancer. For fuck's sake, get me a tighter dress, so I don't have to worry about it coming loose."

She ran off to find something else while I scrolled through my emails. I deleted the junk but noticed an important one: my invite to the

Senator's Gala. It was an annual charity event, which I usually covered, but I would be attending as a guest this year.

This was Senator Banks's first term in office, and he had a soft spot for me—more like a hard spot. I was pretty sure he thought that by inviting me, I would be more willing to go out with him, but he couldn't have been more wrong. I didn't mix business with pleasure. Not that going on a date with him would've been pleasurable. He and I had nothing in common.

His political views differed from mine, and I wouldn't support him. But we didn't discuss these hard-hitting issues. He saw me as a pretty girl who made good arm candy, and that was all I had to offer. However, he had no idea who he was dealing with.

I was well-educated, top of my class at Dartmouth, and I played second-fiddle to no one. If someone wanted to be my equal, I would think about giving them a chance. But no one seemed up for the challenge, so I was more than happy to stay single.

Most people thought I was demanding and too picky. However, I wouldn't lower my standards and settle for less just so I wasn't alone. My own company had been good enough for the last ten years, so why would I change things now?

My career was important to me, but so was my privacy. Since I was already being watched, I didn't need to let random people into my life to give them more fodder to use against me. I was selective for a reason, and it had done me well so far.

I'd landed a spot for Channel 13, the holy grail of stations. I had to work at a few smaller gigs after graduating, but in six short years, I was promoted. Now, I'd been the prime-time anchor for almost seven years. There were even talks of me getting a regional position, which was another reason I needed to be choosy.

As I RSVP'd yes to the Gala, Stacy entered, holding a black pantsuit.

"What is that? I can't go on air wearing something that depressing. I'm covering the new school that's about to open, not someone's funeral. It's spring, so get me something with color. It won't be your job if you can't handle it. Understand?" My voice was bordering on screechy, but I had no tolerance for annoyance, and she'd already crossed the line with her first pick.

"I'm sorry. I thought it would cover you and be diplomatic. But you're right. Some color would be good. What are you going to do with your hair? That will help me decide the perfect outfit."

"If I have to tell you every move to make, I'm better served to cut out the middleman. I think I'll look through the wardrobe myself, and you can take a *long* break?"

"Ms. Starr, please. I can handle it. Give me one more chance?"

I didn't want to be a bitch, but I was in no mood for third chances. Didn't she realize this was strike three? "Stacy, you're dismissed. Thank you for trying."

Her bottom lip quivered, and I couldn't handle seeing her cry, so I called Scott into the room to take care of it.

"Will you please walk Stacy to her car? She will no longer need her keycard or badge, so she needs to return those. Thank you."

Scott had been on security since I'd started here and was my favorite guard. He was a big teddy bear, but you couldn't tell by looking at him. He appeared intimidating at over six feet tall and probably close to two hundred and fifty pounds of muscle. Not to mention, he wore a scowl. But I couldn't fault him for that. I'd been told I had RBF, but I preferred to save my smiles for when I meant them. I grew up in a world full of fake people, which wasn't my style.

After picking out a fuchsia dress with a black belt, I curled my hair to give it a little volume so I could leave it down. As I freshened up my makeup, Scott returned—alone.

"Mon, what did that poor girl do? She's only been with you for two months." His eyes danced with mischief, and I could tell he wanted to smile.

"Seriously? Do I need to remind you of the meme of me? 'Free Titty Committee.'"

He had a belly laugh as he hit the desk with his hand. "Oh. Yeah, but I thought you forgave her for that."

"I did, and then she pulls this shit." I held up the pantsuit with the huge shoulder pads and pleats. "See?"

Studying the outfit, he nodded in agreement. "Ahh. Yeah, that's no bueno. Where did that even come from? Your grandma's closet?"

I laughed, but grandmother had better taste than that. "I'm not sure, but I couldn't handle anymore. What do you think of this?" I stood up and twirled around for him to see the complete ensemble.

He let out a wolf whistle, and I smiled. "You don't even need help. You do a good job on your own."

I knew he was right, but the point was I shouldn't have to do everything on my own. That was one of the perks of working at the bigger station —I would get assistants. If only I could find someone who understood fashion.

"All right. I need to get out there. Could you tell Donavan that I need a new stylist ASAP? I'd prefer to have someone who sews so that they can make me something special for the Gala."

"Oh, yeah. You need to impress your boyfriend," he teased, and I slapped him on his hard chest.

"Please. He wishes. I want something for me—no one else. I don't need anyone's approval."

"Damn right, you don't. Now get your fine self out of here. They're waiting on you."

I walked out to the desk and let the makeup person powder my face to eliminate the shine, and I sat down next to my co-host, Joanna.

"I like that dress. Very eye-catching."

I stared at her, and she was in a white pantsuit, but it was sleek and sleeveless with a V-cut neck. Her hair was pulled back with a few tendrils hanging down, framing her face. She had that girl-next-door thing going on, but she also appeared a little bit like a tomboy. She was around the same age as me, maybe a couple of years older.

I never could read her well, but for the most part, I trusted her. However, I wouldn't say she was in my inner circle. We didn't speak much outside of work.

"Thank you. You look nice as well." It wasn't lip service, but she smirked at my response. I wasn't sure what that meant, but I didn't have time to figure it out as the cameraperson started the countdown.

"We are on in five, four, three..." They held up two and one, then pointed at us.

"Good evening, Atlanta, it is your six o'clock news, and I'm Monica Starr, here with Joanna Wilkinson. Let's take a live look at the new high school opening in the fall. We have Chad on-site with one of the supervisors of the crew..."

I phoned in the rest of the interview as I watched them walk through the halls, and my mind drifted back to my high school days. I'd rather forget those times, but some memories didn't fade.

CHAPTER 3

Jade

PRESENT DAY

Senator Banks was standing on the platform in front of me as I completed the final fitting for the custom suit I had made for the Gala.

"What do you think, sir?" As I kneeled before him, checking the pant length, I noticed a tightening around his crotch.

I didn't understand why he was getting hard, but I jumped back to distance myself from his one-eyed monster.

If his boner embarrassed him, he didn't let on. "They might be a little snug, but what do you think?" He stared at me, and I wasn't sure how to respond.

"Oh? In the waist?" I would have to give him a swift kick if he was hinting at his groin. Surely, he knew how inappropriate it would be to try to solicit sexual favors.

"No. In my thighs."

I bit my lip but refused to bring my eyes down to his legs. "Well, I'm not sure why it would be too tight there. I measured everything before I made them. Have you been doing squats?" I was annoyed, but he was the senator, and I needed this job.

"Could be. Do you think you could measure them again?"

What good would that do? His question made no sense unless he was trying to get me closer to his *thing*. I shuddered, but luck was on my side for once because his phone rang before I had to respond.

"This is Banks," he barked into the receiver. "Oh, hi." His tone was as sweet as pie now. I wondered who he was talking to because I was pretty sure he wasn't married. "I'm happy to hear it. Are you coming as my plus one?"

Maybe it was a blind date type of thing because anyone who met him would realize he was a total skeeze.

"Well, I can help with that." He pulled the phone from his ear. "Hey, what's your name?" He came closer, and I realized he was talking to me.

"I'm... Jade Miller," I stuttered at his unexpected question.

"Right. So, I'm with Jade, and she's an excellent seamstress. She made the suit I'm wearing to the event, and I'm sure she could come up with a dress for you."

What? I didn't have time to make a gown. Did he assume because he was a senator, I would drop everything on my schedule to fit in one of his "first ladies"?

He was out to lunch. I had to put four other clients on hold for him already. No way was I pushing more people back because some naïve woman he wanted to bone needed something to wear.

"Yeah. Okay. She'll be over when she finishes up here. I'm sure you'll be impressed." He hung up the phone, and I was ready to blow my lid, but I swallowed down my anger.

"I'm sorry, sir. Did you offer my services to someone? I appreciate the referral, but I'm on a tight schedule." Hopefully, my fake smile was believable.

"I'll give you three thousand dollars to make Ms. Starr something that compliments me. If she is going to be on my arm, she needs to be the showstopper."

Even though he sounded like an arrogant prick and didn't deserve to have anyone on his arm, I needed the money.

There was no way I could say no, so I nodded like a puppet on a string. "Sounds good. So you said she was ready for me when we finish?"

"Yes. She'll be expecting you at her condo. She's in the Old Fourth Ward. I'll have my assistant text you the details."

With traffic, that would be an extra thirty to forty minutes out of my day, but all I could think about was three thousand dollars.

"Perfect. Thank you for the opportunity. Um..." I'd rather swallow my tongue before saying this, but I had to ask, "Do your pants feel better now that you've moved around in them a little bit?"

He did some lunges, and I worried he might split the seam. I said a silent prayer that he didn't because I couldn't stand the thought of being near him again.

"Actually, yeah. I think they are perfect. Thanks. And make sure Ms. Starr's dress is sexy. I want us to turn heads." He had this desirous look, and I wanted to gag.

"And if you happen to mention how much I paid for your services, I won't be upset. She might appreciate my effort." He winked at me, and I forced myself to smile, but I was pretty sure I came off like a dog baring its teeth.

"All right. Well, I better get going. I don't want to keep her waiting." I let him walk out first so I didn't have to talk to him anymore.

Once he left my shop, I checked my phone and entered the address into Google Maps. I wasn't the best with directions, even though I'd lived here my whole life. The GPS said I would be there in thirty-five minutes, but after hitting the freeway and getting stuck in bumper-to-bumper traffic, it took closer to forty-five.

When I arrived, my jaw dropped. Even though the condos were in the historic part of town, they were obviously brand-new. A privacy fence surrounded the bottom, and a lake with a fountain was in the middle. This place was pretentious, and my ten-year-old Honda didn't fit in.

I rushed out of the car, grabbing my tape measure and notebook, hoping no one saw me. As I walked toward the entrance, I realized I needed to be let in, but I didn't even know the house number or first name of the person I was meeting.

"Great!" What was I going to do? Buzz them all and ask for Ms. Starr? What kind of name was that, anyway? Was she a porn star? I laughed at my joke, even though it wasn't that funny.

As I was thinking of my options, someone approached with a key to get in.

"I'm sorry to bother you. But do you know Ms. Starr?"

He smiled, and I thought he would answer, but he walked right inside, letting the door shut in my face.

"Asshole," I said under my breath as someone else came up.

"He is an asshole. But he respects our privacy, so he's not going to give information to some random person. What are you doing here?"

When I heard that unmistakable voice, I stopped in my tracks. My pulse was racing before I even saw her. Finally getting the nerve to turn around, I was face-to-face with Monica Hart. And somehow, she only got better with age. I couldn't gather a coherent thought, and I braced myself for some snarky comment about the past.

"Yes. I know. I'm on the news. But there's no story here. If you're not a resident, I suggest you go." She didn't recognize me, which shouldn't have been a surprise.

I had changed in the past decade and a half, but so did she. Her skin was still porcelain, but her features were a little softer. I didn't know she was on the news, but the camera probably loved her. My pencil and paper always did.

"Please... move along." She waved her hand, shooing me away.

I shook my head, trying to remember why I was there. "Oh. I'm sorry. I'm here for Ms. Starr. Senator Banks sent me."

She appeared confused, and I wondered if I had the wrong place. Maybe my GPS once again led me astray.

"I'm Ms. Starr." She had a what-the-fuck expression on her face. She thought I recognized her from TV, not high school, and now I felt like an idiot.

Where did that name come from? I guess I wasn't the only one who wanted to reinvent myself.

"Right. I'm Jade... the seamstress. Would it be all right if I came in to take your measurements and discuss your vision? I have several clients I need to finish up with, but the senator is hard to say no to."

She scanned my body, and I could feel the heat creeping up my neck. She wore this gorgeous purple dress that hugged her long, slender frame and hit right above the knee. Black silk ribbon outlined both sides of the V in the neck and then wrapped around her waist in a belt-like fashion. It was intricate detail but simple.

I had on black dress slacks and a white button-down shirt with my sleeves rolled up. She probably thought I had a Charlie Chaplin fetish.

At least this style was a little less dark and angsty than what I wore in high school. Not that she remembered, anyway.

Since the world kissed the ground she walked on, she never took notice of the insignificant peasants.

I stood there, feeling a shiver down my spine as her eyes roamed over me.

"Yeah, you can come inside. But you'll need to leave your cell phone on the table, and there better be no recording devices in your pocket or that bag."

I laughed before I realized she was serious. "Of course. I took my wire off before I got here."

She didn't appear amused as she turned on her heel and raced toward the door. I followed close behind, afraid she would shut me out if I weren't fast enough.

We took the elevator up to the thirteenth floor and went to the last door at the end of the hall. When we walked inside, her place was breathtaking. It was a loft-style with a spiral staircase that led upstairs to what looked like a sitting room with a television and couch. Then I saw two doors off the kitchen to the right and a patio in the back that overlooked the city. It wasn't huge, but the location and the view probably made this place cost more for a month than I would make in a year.

"All right. Cell phone here." She pointed to the table, and I dug it out of my bag and set it down. "What do you need me to do?"

"Well, um, do you know what you want?" I hated that I wasn't more confident, but I couldn't help but feel like that insecure teenager I used to be.

She huffed and let out a huge sigh. "For fuck's sake. That's *your* job. I want a nice dress for a party. Do I need to design it myself? I've already fired one person this week. If I need to let you go, too, I will. You're supposed to come up with the idea and make it. All I'm supposed to do is wear it and look like a badass bitch."

She was more vocal than I remembered, but she still seemed to think she was the prettiest girl in the room. And if I was honest with myself, she was. However, her attitude dropped her down a notch or two.

"Right. Let me take your measurements, and I'll jot down some notes. I want to brainstorm with you, though, because you will be wearing it. So, I can tell you what styles would suit your body type, but in the end, if you're uncomfortable, it won't look as good as it should." I let myself drink her in and hoped she thought I was doing it for research. "Also, your color options will be limited because I've already made Mr. Banks's suit."

"What does that have to do with anything?" Her voice was dripping with annoyance.

Did she not agree to go with him? I'd only heard one side of that conversation, so maybe he had it all wrong.

"He had asked that they coordinate since you were his date." I didn't want to tell her what he said exactly because I didn't want her to feel used.

Although maybe she deserved to know what kind of man she was going out with. I thought of all the times I'd pictured her and me on a date, and I had to laugh. There was no way she'd ever been with a woman if she liked men like that.

"What's so funny?" Her icy stare froze me in place.

Oh no. I'd let my daydream escape to this reality. "Nothing. I was thinking about how nice of a couple you two will make, and I smiled. I wasn't laughing." That excuse was lame to me, but I couldn't change it now.

"Look. I don't know what Trent told you, but I'm *not* accompanying him to the Gala. I am no one's show pony. I want to look good, and it will be for myself."

Wow. That was sexy as hell. Good for her for not conforming for a man.

"Okay. Are these the height of shoes you'll wear?"

She nodded.

I put the tape to the ground and slid my hand up her leg, getting her outseam measurement. Her skin was baby-soft, but I could see tiny goosebumps pop up as my finger grazed her. The blood was rushing in my ears, and I felt dizzy from being so close. Eighteen-year-old me would've been in heaven. Thirty-three-year-old me was about to pass out. I needed to get some air and fast.

CHAPTER 4

Monica

HIGH SCHOOL

"**A**re you wearing Damon's jersey for spirit day?" Tara asked while she slapped on some lip gloss.

I had to fight from rolling my eyes. All she cared about was cheerleading and Damon. I swear she wanted him more than I did.

"I was planning on it. Why? Did you want it?" I shouldn't have been so catty toward her, but sometimes she rubbed me the wrong way.

She only wanted to be my friend for social status, not because she cared about me. None of my friends cared about me. Since my dad was a judge, everyone kissed his ass, and it trickled down the ladder. I was born with people falling all over me, and it got old. I'd never had any real friends.

I wasn't even sure Damon liked me for me. It seemed more like we were together because he was the quarterback and I was the head cheerleader, and everyone shipped us.

"Don't be a biotch. Like I would want your sloppy seconds. I'm wearing Justin's," she said almost under her breath, and I laughed.

Obviously, she wasn't excited because he played soccer, and most students thought soccer was a lesser sport than football. If you asked me,

I didn't care for either of them. In the end, weren't they both "football"?

"Well, that's nice." I could have been more supportive, but being fake was draining.

Just then, the bathroom door opened, and in walked that girl Tara always picked on. I hoped for her sake that Tara was too preoccupied to notice. I tried to make a wall to block Tara's view, but something caught her eye.

"What are you doing in here? This bathroom isn't for losers, *Mistake*." Tara couldn't stop herself from being a bitch, and I wanted to tell her to shut the fuck up, but I wasn't going to start a fight with my "friend" for some girl I didn't know.

I knew Damon had a soft spot for her, but I wasn't as strong as him. He could take the heat for it, but I didn't think I could. Aargh, that sounded selfish even to me, but I didn't feel like I had a choice. Everyone had these expectations of me, and hanging out with the outcasts wasn't it. Maybe I could do something to take Tara's attention away from her.

"Tara! You have to see this." I called her over, and she stopped mid-sentence about the poor girl being a devil worshiper.

It was uncalled for, but there were worse things she could have said.

As she rushed over to me and stared, I realized I didn't have anything to show her. "What am I looking at?" she questioned.

"Oh? This." I pointed to a non-existent spot on my cheek. "I think I have a pimple forming." While I kept Tara busy, I glanced over her head and gave an imperceptible nod to Mystique, and she seemed to understand what I was doing and left.

"Yeah, I see it. Yikes. Do you want some of my concealer?" She was almost giddy at the thought of me breaking out.

I examined my face closer, which was clear, but I played along for appearance's sake. "Please? You're a lifesaver."

She pulled out her tube and handed it to me. "Where did Mistake go? I wasn't done asking her if she drank blood as a ritual or just for fun." She cackled like the wicked witch she was.

"Why don't you lay off of her?" I didn't mean to let the words slip out, but it was how I felt.

"Why do you care so much? Do you and Damon both have a thing for her?"

Damon had a thing for her? Huh. Maybe he did, and that was why he always offered her rides. That would be an interesting turn of events: star quarterback slumming it with the lonely goth girl.

I wasn't sure why she wanted to look like that. She had decent features —nice eyes, high cheekbones, and very pouty lips. I wished my lips were as full as hers. If she didn't dye her hair dark blue and wear it hanging over her face, where all you could see was the black lipstick, people might give her a chance. But she must have enjoyed the ridicule, or else she'd try to fit in better.

"Whatever. Damon and I are pleased with our relationship." I mean, we sort of were happy, I guess.

Many things were going on in my life that kept me busy. Besides that, I was very content by myself. Damon wasn't a bad guy. He just didn't do much for me. We'd dated since sophomore year, so this was like our farewell tour. We would break up as soon as we graduated, but for now, he was someone to pass the time with. However, he wasn't someone I longed to be around.

He sweated profusely for no reason at all. His hands were rough, but he always wanted to hold mine, and it felt like a scouring pad against my skin. I knew lots of girls would have fallen over themselves to have him touch them, but that wasn't me.

Tara would probably give her left tit to be in my situation: I was captain of the cheerleading squad, dating a football player, and I had all the right connections.

I realized I was fortunate. Everything seemed to fall into my lap, but I'd never asked for it. And if it was something I wanted, I worked hard—like cheerleading.

"Oh really? Why did I see him talking to Libby the other day?" Since she wasn't happy, she didn't want anyone else to be.

"Because he doesn't belong to me, and he can speak to whomever he wants." I swore she wanted something to throw in my face.

"Well, if he were *my* boyfriend, I wouldn't let him anywhere near the school slut."

"Jeez, Tara. You don't have to speak so rudely about people. And you won't ever have to worry about him being *your* boyfriend because he and I are endgame." Even though I knew it wasn't true, she didn't, and I needed to drop her down a peg.

She was getting too comfortable in this "my shit doesn't stink" role. "Whatevs. I'm over this. Let's go to lunch." She stared at me as if I should jump up and follow her, but I was no one's puppet.

"I'll be there in a second. I have some stuff to take care of. It's that time..."

"Oh. That explains a lot. I thought you were being a bitch for no reason." As she headed out the door, I stopped myself from giving her the finger in case she had eyes in the back of her head.

I wasn't actually on my period, but I couldn't stand her thinking she was in charge. As I stared into the mirror, I touched up my makeup, even though I didn't need to. Then I took out my brush and pulled my hair in a high pony. When I decided I'd killed enough time, I walked out, only to run face-first into Goth Girl.

"Watch where you're going." My tone was much harsher than I intended.

She appeared as scared as a feral cat as her eyes darted this way and that. "Sorry. I thought it was empty. I'll come back later."

"It's fine. I'm leaving." But before the door shut, I held it open and asked, "Why do you let people pick on you? You could be normal if you wanted to. I don't get it."

Something in her face changed, and she no longer appeared skittish but composed. "Who decides what 'normal' is? I'll find my people one day when I'm out of this fish bowl. And I've accepted that it won't be in high school."

Well, good on her. But I wouldn't choose that life. I let the door close and headed to the cafeteria to face the sea of sharks and wondered if I'd ever be as brave as she was.

CHAPTER 5

Jade

PRESENT DAY

"**M**ay I step out on the patio?" I didn't know if that would help, but I needed space.

Her silky skin was sending my body into overdrive. If I had stayed that close to her, I couldn't have been responsible for what I might have done. She was wearing a short dress, and it wouldn't have taken much for me to bury my face between her legs. Oh my God. Those thoughts needed to leave my head. Without waiting for a response, I rushed to the door.

"Yeah, sure. Be careful—"

Whack. I ran right into the unforgiving glass. The pain shot from my face through my body, all the way down to my stubbed toe.

"The door sticks." She finished her thought, but it was too late.

"Yeah, I see that." I touched my nose, and I didn't think it was broken. At least it wasn't bleeding.

She came over, holding a towel with some ice in it. "Here. Do you need some aspirin or anything? You smacked into it pretty hard. It was like you were trying to escape a fire."

She was sort of right. Only I couldn't outrun the flames because they came from within.

She reached up and gently touched her hand against my nose. "It's already bruised a little. The ice should help. Do you still want to go outside?" Her tone was the softest I'd ever heard, and she probably thought she had to be friendly, or I might bail.

"Um, if you don't mind. I think the fresh air will do me some good."

Her chest brushed against my back as she reached around me and turned the knob before giving the door a good thump with her hip.

"All right. But I have other things to do today, so if you could hurry, I'd appreciate it." She was back to her no-nonsense.

"Of course." Scooting out to the patio, I took deep breaths and let the wind cool off my skin. It was spring, so the humidity wasn't high yet, and I felt myself relaxing.

"You ready?" she barked out, and all my tension immediately returned.

"Coming." I rushed inside to find her standing in her bra and panties. My eyes darted all over her body, but I finally lowered my head to avoid a panic attack. Surely this wasn't happening? "What are you doing? Why are you naked?"

"What? I'm not naked. I know you have to finish my measurements, so I thought I would save you the hassle of asking me to take off my dress. So... can we continue? I want to go to a Pilates class in forty-five minutes."

She had always appeared slender in high school, but now that I could see her without any barriers, she was toned. I mentally traced the lines in her body and could tell she worked out. The corner of my mouth hitched, and I swallowed hard.

"Yes. Yeah. Sure. I'll get right on it." Feeling like a fumbling idiot, I reached for my tape measure and dropped it.

I went to pick it up, but so did she, and I was face-to-tits. Her breasts weren't big, but they were perfect. They were round and perky, and I imagined what they looked like under the bra. I wasn't sure if she realized I had already grabbed the tape or if she'd caught me staring at her chest, but she popped back into position, ready for me to continue.

She clapped her hands. "All right. Let's get with it."

I slid her feet apart and trailed a finger up the inside of her leg to get her inseam. Her smooth skin was begging to be touched, but I kept it professional—at least in real life, but I had no control over my thoughts. I then took circumference measurements—starting with her calf and working my way up to her knee. When I got to the fullest part of her thigh, I had to bite my lip to keep from letting out an appreciative "hmmm."

"So, have you always wanted to design clothes?" She must not like the awkward silence because I highly doubted she cared about my aspirations.

I let out the breath I was holding so I could respond. "I didn't know what I wanted to do until I got to college. I used to sketch a lot, and I thought being an artist would be fun. But I took a couple of drawing classes, and the teacher offered job ideas, and fashion design was one of them. So I enrolled in a sewing course, and the rest is history."

"Interesting," she said but didn't sound amused.

As I stood up to measure her crotch area, I made eye contact before placing the tape at the top of her waist in the front. It was awkward as I moved it between her legs and up to the center of her waist in the back.

I wasn't sure if she was nervous, but it looked like her chest was rising and falling faster. "Could you stay straight, please?"

"I am straight," she snapped back at me, and I could see little red blotches around her chest and neck.

Maybe I was oversensitive since I was gay, but that seemed pointed. "Right. Well, I have several more measurements to get. Are you okay if I continue?" The last thing I wanted was to cause weirdness between us.

"Yes. Get what you have to, then get out."

So much for the small talk. I could tell something had shifted, but I didn't know what. If she thought I was calling her gay, I definitely wasn't. My mind may have wished that for the past fifteen years, but I was a realist and knew she didn't speak in tongues.

Her animosity must have been a sign of her discomfort. I worked quickly, getting the rest of the numbers so I could get out of there. It suddenly felt frigid, and I didn't need to deal with this hostility. I'd done nothing wrong, but I somehow felt like a predator by doing my job.

"All right. I have everything. If you could take a couple of minutes to send me some designs you feel the most confident in, I'll come up with something for you. And if you're sure you're not going with Mr. Banks, let me know which colors you like best." I handed her my card, and she took it while covering her chest with her other arm.

"Yeah, that's fine. I'll email you tonight."

No other words were traded, and I walked out feeling confused and hurt.

When I got to my car, I typed in the location of Joe Joe's Café and texted Iris to see if she could meet me.

Iris: Of course. Now? Haley put the twins down, so it's a good time.

Me: Thanks. See you in 30.

Iris: Thumbs-up emoji

For some reason, seeing Monica had brought up feelings I wasn't sure how to deal with. Iris was one of my closest friends and an excellent listener, so I figured if anyone could help me, it was her.

After parking the car, I got out and walked toward the entrance at the same time Iris was.

"Hey. Fancy seeing you." She smiled and wrapped me in a quick hug before opening the door. "What's going on? You seem down."

We stood in line, and I tried to explain what was bothering me.

"I'm not sure. I had a weird encounter with a blast from the past, and I'm feeling off-kilter now."

"Next," the cashier called out.

"Um, I'll have a nitro cold brew and..." I nodded my head toward Iris.

"No. I can get my own." She waved me off.

"Is that all then?" The guy appeared annoyed.

"She'll have a Venti caffé latte with extra foam," I responded without giving her a chance to argue.

Iris quirked her eyebrow, but I knew what she liked.

"All right. That's $10.58. Can I have your names, please?"

"The cold brew is Jade, and the latte is Iris," I answered and offered a smile, but he didn't return the niceties.

"I can help who's next," he called out, and we stepped away from the counter.

"So, how are the babies?" I asked nonchalantly, but she could see I was deflecting.

"They are good. Haven't changed much since you saw them last week." She winked at me teasingly.

"Okay. Well, I'm glad everything is good."

"Tell me why you texted. Who is this blast from the past, and what do they have to do with this..." she waved her hand in front of me, "bad aura?"

"Jade. Iris." The barista set our coffees on the counter, and we picked them up before taking a seat.

"Well, it's a long story, I guess."

"Okay. I have about an hour before the twins wake up. I'm all yours until then."

CHAPTER 6

Monica

PRESENT DAY

As soon as the seamstress left, I dressed for my Pilates class, but I was feeling agitated. I wasn't sure why, but I hoped the exercise would relieve the tension building in my neck.

Once I arrived at Studio 303, I checked my makeup in the rearview before entering. I knew it was stupid to be in full-face to work out, but I always had to be on. It was exhausting, but it was a small price to pay for having the job of my dreams.

After finding a place at the bar, I started stretching and watched in the mirror as more people arrived. The class was full, which slightly annoyed me because I enjoyed having a little more space. When Chad, the instructor, walked in, everyone faced the front, and all the girls swooned.

He was good-looking in that obvious sort of way with the chiseled jaw and shaggy hair that hung a little over his eyes, but he honestly didn't do much for me. I hadn't been serious with anyone since college, and even then, Jamison was more of the "good on paper" type than someone I wanted to spend my life with.

With my dad on the Bench, my partner had certain expectations to meet. My father was a conservative, and even though my views didn't align with his, I couldn't be caught dating a "liberal." So, I was chained to uptight fuddy-duddies who sparked as much passion inside me as hugging a cactus would.

It was probably why I enjoyed being single because I couldn't stand being fake. I'd spent my earlier life living in a plastic world. At least now, I could be me without putting on airs for anyone. If I focused on my career, I didn't have to worry about my lack of social life. I always had Scott and Tina, from work, who I could hang out with if I got bored, but curling up with a good book was my idea of fun.

I lay on the mat as Chad guided us through breathing and felt some of my uneasiness floating away. As I inhaled deeply, I closed my eyes, but someone pressing on my stomach disrupted my peace.

"Hold it in." Chad's voice caused my eyes to pop open, and he was now straddling my legs. His fingers moved right beneath my breasts, and the air escaped my lungs as I pushed him off. "Whoa." He stumbled back and held his hands up in surrender.

People were staring now, but he just moved on to his next more than willing participant. I realized I might have been too sensitive, but I wasn't comfortable with anyone in my space. At least I hadn't been before Jade. A shiver ran through my body. Something about her touch was weirdly familiar yet new and exciting.

What the hell was I thinking? It wasn't like she was there to cop a feel. She was fitting me for a dress. How pathetic was I? Not only that, but why was I thinking of *her*?

The only people I'd dated in my life were men. Women usually competed with me. I never saw them as potential lovers.

In all fairness, I never pictured myself with anyone. Most of the time, it seemed like people were more trouble than they were worth. That was a bleak outlook, but my experience shaped my point of view.

As I went through the rest of the class on autopilot, I was still a little perturbed by my thoughts of Jade. They were probably from all the drama I dealt with today, but they were still unsettling. I rolled up my mat and was on my way out of class when Chad stopped me.

"Hey. I didn't mean anything by it. I was trying to help you with your breathing. I hope you don't think I was..." he looked around to make sure no one was in earshot, then mouthed, "sexually harassing you."

"Of course not. I'm jumpy, that's all. I'm sorry for the knee-jerk reaction. You were doing your job." That was a little bit of bullshit. I didn't see why he needed to come up that high on my body, but at the same time, there was no need to ruin his reputation over it.

He smiled brightly and probably thought it would win me over, but he was sadly mistaken.

"Well, I'm glad you came to class, and maybe I'll see you sometime outside of here." He ran a hand through his hair and then shook his head to get the bangs out of his eyes.

Was he seriously flirting with me? Guys could be so daft sometimes.

"Stranger things have happened." I threw my towel over my shoulder and walked out.

When I got outside, my stomach growled, and I realized it was 2:00 p.m., and I hadn't eaten since breakfast. I didn't have a long time before I had to be on set, so I needed to grab something quickly. Looking over at Joe Joe's Café, I figured I could get a scone to tide me over until I got to the station. I never had food at home because I didn't cook.

I rushed inside and stood in line, tapping my foot. At least three people were in front of me, and I hated nothing more than waiting.

I scanned the place, making sure no one noticed me. The last thing I wanted was a sweaty picture of me floating around. Even though I was put together better than most people after a workout, I didn't feel picture-worthy at the moment. However, I didn't see any cameras on me, but I spotted something else that caught my eye—*Jade*.

I hunkered down, so she couldn't see me. She was sitting with some woman, laughing and seeming pretty cozy. Maybe they were on a date. The thought made me uneasy.

I wasn't sure why, but I assumed she was single. Not that it mattered. I wasn't interested in her—was I? Who was I kidding? I didn't even know her.

As I studied the two of them, someone pushed me from behind. "Hey, are you going to move up in the line?"

I turned toward him. "I'm not even next, but please, go ahead." I gave a sweeping motion with my hand before continuing my spying.

I wished I could get close enough to hear what they were talking about, but I knew there was no chance of that. Maybe I could read their lips if I squinted. While trying my best to get intel, my shield moved, exposing me.

"Next," the guy behind the counter called out.

I scooted forward and noticed Jade had turned her head this way. Grabbing a menu, I held it in front of my face.

"Do you know what you want?" he asked.

"Um, yeah, a blueberry scone, please. And decaf Americano."

"Okay. That's $8.73. Are you the lady from the news?"

Oh shit. "What? No. I have to go. Cancel that." I ran out of the café, hoping no one saw, especially Jade.

As I stood on the sidewalk, holding that damn menu, I was left with the dilemma of taking it back in or just stealing it. Aha. I had a better idea. Someone was walking inside.

"Excuse me, sir." I stopped him.

He stared at me for a second with wandering eyes. "Do I know you?"

"Me? No? I'm nobody. I just had an airhead moment and walked out with this menu. Since I'm in a hurry, I was hoping you could take it in with you?"

A grin played across his lips, and his hand caressed mine as he grabbed the menu. "Sure, Doll. Have a good day."

I had to pry out of his grip and keep myself from showing my disgust. After giving him my best politician smile, I rushed to my car. My stomach was still growling, but it didn't matter because I had to get the hell out of dodge.

I drove home and raided my condo only to find a box of stale crackers, which, much to my chagrin, I ate an entire sleeve of them. After showering, I blow-dried my hair and threw on some joggers and a T-shirt to head down to the station.

Even though I didn't go on air until 6:00 p.m., I had to get there with enough time to get dressed and fix my hair and makeup. Without a stylist, I would need to do everything myself, and I wasn't sure if that would take longer, so I left early.

When I walked in, the first person I saw was Scott, and he quirked an eyebrow at me.

"Hey, Ms. Starr. You're looking flushed today."

That wasn't what I needed to hear right now. I ignored him and headed to my dressing room.

"Oh no, you don't." He was quick on my heels as he grabbed my arm. "Did you get laid?"

"Scott! That is entirely inappropriate." I smacked him upside his chest.

"And it's true, or you wouldn't be as red as a monkey's ass." He let out a deep, throaty laugh, and I was taken aback.

"What? Monkey's asses are red?"

"I don't know. It's a saying. I didn't make it up." He shrugged, and I stared at him quizzically.

At least we were on a different subject. "Interesting. I wonder if there are other animals with red asses."

"Why would you wonder that?"

"I don't know. Why did you bring it up in the first place?" Shit. Now I circled back to the topic I didn't want to discuss.

35

"Because your face was as red as it. Meaning—you got laid." He pointed at me, and I slapped his finger away.

"Scott! It means no such thing. If I'm red in the face, it's because I did Pilates and had to rush here right after. As soon as I get into hair and makeup, I'll be good as new."

"Okay. Say I buy that. Why are you jumpy about the sex thing? I tell you when I score."

The fact that he called it "scoring" annoyed me. Scott and I were friends outside of here. He was one of very few, but I never thought of sex as a game. It was just something people did. Was it pleasurable—sometimes. Was it worth bragging about—never.

"Yeah, but I don't ask you. That information is volunteered. And I'm not telling you anything about my personal life. You know that my lips are sealed." I mimed a zipping motion over my mouth, and he rolled his eyes.

"All right, Ms. Starr. I'll leave you to it. But don't think I won't get to the bottom of this after the segment." He pointed to his eyes and then mine before returning to his post.

I hated that he called me Ms. Starr, but his boss made it mandatory for all the guards to use our last names—regardless of what we wanted. He was old school like that.

When I got into my room, a dress and shoes were already laid out, and someone was rummaging through the racks.

"Hello?" I questioned, and a person popped into view. My heart dropped into my stomach.

"Oh. Hey. Our good friend, the senator, called and informed me you needed a stylist for the show tonight, and he offered to pay me handsomely. His words, not mine. Anyway, I had already canceled my clients for the day, so here I am." Jade smiled as she continued to sort through the clothes.

"How did he know I needed a stylist? Why would *he* pay you? The show pays for that." None of this made any sense.

36

"I'm going to guess the same reason why he paid for your dress—he thinks it will impress you. How he knew..." she shrugged her shoulders. "But I could use the extra cash, so I took him up on the deal."

Interesting. He wanted to buy his way into my pants? Ha! That would never happen. But judging by the outfit Jade chose for me, I was glad he was stupid enough to think it would work. She knew my style better than I did and seemed to know what she was doing.

I studied her hands while she laid out a few options for me. They were strong yet feminine, and I couldn't stop remembering her soft touch as her fingers had crept up my legs earlier.

"So, this is what I was thinking." Her voice pulled me out of a daydream, and I felt heat rushing to my face.

"There's nothing to think about. This outfit is fine. You're dismissed." I was such a bitch, but I didn't want to have any more unsolicited thoughts floating around, and her being this close to me was about to do my head in.

"Wow. I guess I won't discuss your dress for the Gala." She closed her eyes, and I worried she was fighting back tears.

I didn't want to make her cry, but I was trying to protect myself. I reached out, touching her shoulder, but she flinched as if I'd slapped her.

"What is your problem? You're not the fucking Queen of England who can *dismiss* the peasants. You might have reigned in high school, but we're adults now. The playing field is level. So if you want me to help you, you'll treat me with respect. I don't care who you are. You're not better than me."

Oh. She wasn't going to cry. She was biting her tongue. And How did she know what I was like in high school? Regardless, her standing up to me was... No one did that, and I liked it. Oh my fucking God! I *liked* it?

I studied her pale-blue eyes, which were innocent yet fierce-looking, and I could tell she meant business. I needed someone like her in my life to keep me in check.

"Be my stylist full-time." It wasn't a question because I didn't want to give her the option to say no.

"What?" She rubbed her temples as if she were getting a migraine. "Are you even listening? I said I want respect, and then you *tell* me to work for you? Hard pass."

She sighed, and I was about to plead my case, but apparently, she was just getting started. "I have my own shop. I was doing this one time for extra cash because I eventually want to start a clothing line. But I won't give up my dream because you beckoned me. I'm not your minion. You don't control me."

The confidence in her tone had my insides dancing. Most people I could take or leave. But her... I wanted her to stay.

I realized I would have to swallow my pride and use a different approach if I wanted to keep her. "You're right. I was being an ass. I would be grateful if you would work *with* me, not for me."

She appeared skeptical, and I needed a better pitch, or I would lose her.

"And You wouldn't just be my stylist, you could also design my clothes."

That seemed to arouse her interest, so I continued. "I would be more than willing to wear your stuff on TV and even give you a free plug now and then. What do you say? You could still work toward your dream, but you'd help me, too. It's a win-win." I offered a genuine smile that reached my eyes, and I could tell she was softening to it. I grabbed both of her shoulders and stared directly at her. "Jade, please? Let's be partners?"

She covered her face with her hands and groaned but slowly nodded, and I knew I'd won her over.

"Yeah?" I asked to make sure I was reading the signs.

"Okay. But if you fuck up once. I'm out. I will not be treated like a child. We are *partners*, or we're nothing. Got it?"

She drove a hard bargain, but she had no idea what I would do to keep her. I'd never felt this alive, and I didn't want to lose it.

CHAPTER 7

Jade

HIGH SCHOOL

I t was seventh period, and school was almost over. I was finishing a sketch I'd started at lunch of Monica sitting on the promenade with the sun shining down on her tanned skin. She had a book in her hand and appeared peaceful. I couldn't help but draw her—she was my greatest muse.

"All right, class dismissed. Have a good weekend." Mrs. Neumeyer smiled brightly as everyone began filing out.

After sliding my notebook into my bag, I stood up only to have someone slam into me.

"Sorry, not sorry," Tara said as she pushed her way to Damon. She wrapped her arm through his like she was claiming him.

"What are you doing?" he asked as he shook her off.

"Nothing. I wanted to see if you were going to the party tonight?" She batted her eyelashes, but he didn't appear to notice.

She was flirting with him, and it was sad she would do that to Monica. They were supposed to be best friends. But at the same time, it wouldn't be the end of the world to me if Monica were single. I had to laugh at myself for even thinking that would change how she saw me. To

Monica, I would always be nothing—a nobody. But if she only knew how I saw her, maybe...

"What are you looking at, freak?" Tara spat at me, and I realized I had zoned out while staring at her and Damon.

"I'm sorry. I was leaving." I started to walk by, but she stuck her foot out, and I stumbled. Luckily, Damon caught me, stopping me from face-planting. "Thank you." I kept my head down to hide my embarrassment.

"Why don't you take a hike, Tara?" He pulled me upright and kept his arm around my shoulder. "Are you okay?" He asked, and I could see why Monica was smitten with him. He was sweet and protective, and I would even have to say cute—if you liked that boyish-charming thing, which I didn't, but he was perfect for someone who did—Monica.

"Oh my God. What's your problem? You're going to choose Wednesday Addams over me? You and Monica need to get a life and stop trying to be a savior all the time." Tara spun on her heel and darted off, leaving us with his arm wrapped around me.

"Thank you." This time I looked him in the eyes when I said it. "But you don't have to stick up for me. I'll be okay."

He grabbed both of my shoulders, squaring my body to his. "I know that. But I like you, Mystique. You don't give a fuck what anyone else thinks about you, and well..."

Before he could finish that thought, Monica strolled in, and I pulled out of his grip.

"What's Tara's deal? I heard her mumble something about you thinking you could save the lost souls?" She didn't appear concerned that her boyfriend had his hands on me a few seconds ago. In fact, she never showed much emotion at all.

I honestly didn't know what it was about her that consumed me. She wasn't the nicest person, and she let Tara bully everyone without even batting an eyelash. Then I stared at her long eyelashes, and my eyes dropped to her lips, which always looked soft and shiny—kissable.

40

I'd only kissed one person, and that was my best friend, Aaron, so to say it wasn't movie-worthy was an understatement. But I could imagine kissing her and how it would probably make fireworks go off.

"Who knows with her? She has a stick up her ass." Damon reached out his hand for Monica's. She hesitated for a second before taking it and smiling.

"You ready?" She tugged him a little closer, and I scooted out of the way.

He cocked his head toward me. "You need a lift?"

"Oh, no. I'm okay." I didn't want to be a charity case, but I wanted to take him up on the offer. My heart was racing as I remembered the last time I rode with them, and Monica's thigh pressed against mine.

"Come on. I don't want you to walk. There's room, right, Mon?"

Her expression appeared annoyed, but she nodded. "Of course," she said, tight-lipped.

I could tell she didn't want me to go, but the words were out of my mouth before I could think clearly. "Okay. I appreciate it."

"Any time." Damon reached out to me, and I glanced at Monica, who didn't seem to notice.

I wasn't sure if I should take his hand, but I did. His skin was calloused and a little sweaty, but it was nice to feel safe. Monica was lucky to have that comfort from someone. I only wished it could come from me and not him.

We walked through the empty hallway as a triad, but secretly I pictured it as a twosome—Monica and me. I bet her skin was as smooth as butter and not clammy.

Damon was so good to me and didn't deserve me fantasizing about his girlfriend. But my mind did what it wanted without any say-so from me.

When we made it to the truck, we piled in like last time. Before I could even sit down, Monica's legs were on my side. I couldn't tell if she was

41

trying to keep me out or... I let myself believe she wanted to touch me, too.

Sliding in, I brushed against her thigh, and desire was pooling at my center. She was wearing a skirt, and her legs were open, and I could picture gliding my fingers up her soft skin and burying them deep inside of her.

Oh, sweet baby Jesus. I had to get rid of those thoughts. "Sorry. I didn't mean to bump into you."

"It's fine. This truck is small." And like last time, her arm went behind me, and I pretended she wanted me the way I wanted her.

(Present Day)

My alarm went off, and my heart beat wildly inside its cage. Remembering the way Monica made me feel wouldn't make being around her every day any easier. I never should have taken this job. But she seemed so sincere in wanting me there, and my younger self would kick my ass if I turned it down.

Getting dressed today seemed different than it had before. I usually wore slacks and a button-down shirt, but they always said to dress for the job you want, not the one you have. And I wanted to apply for the role of her girlfriend. I knew it wasn't one I would ever fill, but maybe I could wish it to fruition. I would never know if I didn't try.

I picked out a black jumpsuit I had made with a double-breasted waist that looked like a cummerbund and straps that were mock suspenders. It was wide-legged, and I paired it with a white button-down shirt, leaving the top four buttons open. I had a smaller chest, so there wasn't any fear of them popping out. But maybe the little bit of skin would cause some ideas to float in her head.

Before I left the house, I brushed my hair, but it never made a difference. It was short, and I tucked it behind my ears anyway. However, I hoped my effort wouldn't go unnoticed.

I got in my car and drove down to my shop. I didn't have to be at the studio until 4:00 p.m., so I could still take care of some of my other clients, which was perfect for me because they were loyal customers, and I didn't want to blow them off.

When I arrived, I set my stuff down and began working on the alterations for a suit. I only had to hem the legs and tuck in the waist, which wouldn't take me long, but it was one of the tedious tasks I didn't enjoy as much as drawing and creating. However, it was those simpler jobs that paid the bills.

As I wrapped up the final stitch, my phone beeped, and I went to check my messages.

Iris: Hey. Curious how the dress for your lover was coming. She added the crying laughing emoji, and I wished I'd never told her about Monica.

I hadn't talked to Iris since I left the coffee shop, so she had no idea we were working together now, and I thought it better to keep that to myself for the time being. She probably would have frowned upon me putting myself right in the thick of things, knowing I would never be more than Monica's "friend," and I used that word loosely.

Me: You're so funny. I haven't started on it yet, but once I finish it, you can model it for me.

Iris was more of a tomboy than me, so her in a gown would be as weird as seeing a fish walk.

Iris: We both seem to be comedians today. Good luck with everything, and keep me posted!

Me: Will do! Tell Haley and the twins hi.

She messaged back a smiley face with hearts on it, and I tucked my phone away to get back to work. As I laid the fabric on the machine, my phone rang. I couldn't believe Iris was calling. But when I picked it up, I saw Monica's name across the caller ID.

"Why?" I said to myself, but I felt like my only option was to answer. "Hello?"

"Jade. It's Monica. I need you to come in around 3:00 this afternoon instead of 4:00. I have some ideas I want to run by you about my dress, and if you could grab me a coffee and a scone on the way, that would be great. Get whatever you want, too." She sounded serious, but this had to be a joke.

"I'm sorry. Do you think I'm your assistant?" I thought we were *partners*, but I should have known.

"No! I thought you wanted to talk to me about dress ideas. The event is in two months, and I'm sure I'll need to try it on and have enough time to come up with something else if it doesn't work."

So now she was already assuming that what I did wouldn't be satisfactory? Why did she even want me to help her then?

"Listen. If you're afraid my outfit will be shit, why did you practically beg me to work with you?"

She scoffed into the phone. "I most certainly did *not* beg you. And I never said your designs were bad. I was merely being realistic that not everything works on the first try. I feel you're out to make me a villain when all I'm trying to do is help you achieve your dream."

Was that all she was doing? Because from what I remembered of her, she didn't do much unless it was for her benefit. But I knew we were older, and people changed, so I would give her another chance.

"I'm sorry. I guess I'm sensitive to better-than-thou people." It came across as a dig, but I didn't necessarily mean it that way.

"And you think that's me? I can't help how I appear to others, but I've never once thought I was better than anyone."

My years in high school begged to differ, but that was neither here nor there. She didn't even remember me, so I should count this as a starting over point. Let that be water under the bridge and get to know her now. Like everyone else, I always had her on a pedestal, but it was time to bring her down with the rest of us. She might have looked the same, but maybe she was humble and kind now.

I thought back to Damon and how he was the only person in that clique of popular people who ever stood up for me. Maybe she stayed with him after high school, and some of his characteristics rubbed off on her. Then I started thinking about how I would like to rub off on her, and I knew I had to end this conversation quickly.

"You're right. I was being unfair. I can meet you at 3:00 today, but next time, ask—don't tell me."

"Of course. I'm sorry. So, will you still be able to pick up my coffee and scone?"

"I'll see you at 3:00."

"Was that a—"

I hung up the phone before she could put her foot farther in her mouth. That woman had a lot of nerve. I'd give her that. I had to chuckle, though, because she was utterly oblivious to how the world worked. Maybe I could help her see things more clearly. Sometimes all we needed was a different perspective.

CHAPTER 8

Monica

PRESENT DAY

I couldn't believe it. Jade hung up on me. Why did that have my stomach doing somersaults? Did I like that she was defiant? No one ever questioned me like her, and something about that pleased me. It was like the challenge excited me. That was weird. Didn't most people love getting their way?

I didn't have time to ponder what I felt because I'd already called her in early but didn't have anything to discuss. Since I'd told her I did, I had to get in gear. I grabbed an old fashion magazine to see if I could find some inspiration.

As I flipped through some pages, I came across Elizabeth Hurley at the premiere of *Four Weddings and a Funeral* and knew I had found something I would love to wear. The dress had a plunging neckline, a thigh-high slit, and the sides held together with safety pins. It would be cool enough for the summer heat, but some adjustments would need to be made.

I was sure Jade could come up with something to make it a little dressier. Maybe a different fabric or a see-through sheathing to cover the skin. I guess it wasn't my job to decide, but I felt like this was a good place to start.

I would look like a rock star, and hopefully, Jade would be able to launch her career on that dress. Even though I'd never seen anything she'd done personally, she was self-assured and poised, which made me believe she was good. At least she had good taste. Yesterday, I'd gotten probably fifteen compliments on my outfit before I even made it to the stage. I was used to people telling me what they thought I wanted to hear, but this felt different. They seemed... genuine.

Now that I had an idea, I felt better about her coming in early. If I'd shown up empty-handed, she would've seen through my flimsy excuse and figured out I just wanted to see her.

She had this mysterious side that I needed to uncover. She appeared shy at times, but then she would turn around and take the bull by the horns. The dichotomy had my mind spinning. But what twisted me up the most was how she made me feel inside.

I'd gone on maybe two handfuls of first dates and half as many second dates since graduating college, and not one of those men sparked my desire. In fact, the more they talked and the closer they got to me, the less I liked them. I'd thought I loved my only two serious boyfriends, Damon and Jamison, but ultimately, I was let down.

The time I'd spent with Jade already made me feel more than either of them did, and it confused the hell out of me. I'd never thought I was attracted to women. In all actuality, I never had a strong sexual pull to anyone. But she seemed to camp out in my mind, and I didn't know how to get rid of her.

She was unique with her dark-red hair that she tucked behind her ears. And those oceans for eyes. They looked so innocent but knowing at the same time. Like she'd been in the trenches but came out stronger. I wanted to know more about her, but my life didn't afford me the luxury to let many people in. So, I would have to settle for keeping her in my orbit but only in the peripheral.

If I kept thinking of Jade, I would drive myself mad, so I grabbed my phone and called my mom. It had been a few weeks, and if I didn't do it soon, I would get some severe guilt trips.

The phone rang twice before she picked up.

"Katherine speaking."

She had to know it was me, yet she still answered the same way.

"Hey, Mom. I thought I would check on you and Daddy to see how things were going."

She exhaled loudly into the receiver, which almost hurt my ear. "Well, things are tense, if I'm honest."

Of course they were. If everything wasn't perfect, she thought the world was ending.

"I'm sorry to hear that. Is Daddy home?" Sometimes my dad could be easier to handle because he was more of a straight-shooter and didn't drag out all the unnecessary details.

"No. He's at the Club with the new District Attorney. Did I tell you who that was?"

I honestly didn't care, but I couldn't fake as I knew, so I had to play along. "No?"

"That boy you dated in high school—Damon Goodson. Did you know he's married with two children? You missed the boat on that one, but I'm sure we can find you someone suitable. However, you might be past your prime for children. I would use a surrogate."

I would've rather had the guilt trip than listen to this nonsense. I didn't miss any boat. Damon dumped me because he had feelings for someone else. Not that it mattered because I didn't feel much for him either. I mean, he was my first, but I wouldn't say he set my world on fire.

And I wasn't too old to have kids. It just so happened that I didn't want children, so that was a moot point. But I knew I would have to settle down soon, or people would start to think I was the Judge's spinster daughter who couldn't land a man because she was too frigid. I'd heard that comment before.

The thought of someone encroaching on my space made my skin crawl. I didn't need anyone to make me happy. I found contentment in my work and within myself. But sometimes, I felt on autopilot as I navigated through life. Maybe I needed to get out more and do things that took me out of my comfort zone.

"I'm not worried about a timetable. I'm working on my career, and I honestly couldn't be happier for Damon and his family. He was always a nice guy." That was true. I never held any ill will toward him.

"Oh, he's nice, all right..." her voice got lower, "To look at. But don't you tell your father I said that." She laughed, and I knew she was kidding, but I still didn't want to think of her ogling my ex—it was weird.

"Well, I hate to cut this conversation short, but I must get ready for work. I have to go in early for a meeting. Tell Daddy hi, and I love you both." I made a kissy noise.

"All right, dear. Have a good day. I can't wait to watch you. Oh, before you go, your dress was stunning yesterday. I hope you wear something as nice tonight. You'd hate to drop from the top. It would be a long way down."

"Thanks, Mom. I'll talk to you soon." I disconnected the call and hoped that would hold her over for a couple of weeks.

Even though my parents only lived about thirty minutes from me, I tried to keep my visits through the phone and only make the in-person ones when necessary.

I checked the clock, and it was only noon. I already had all my stuff done for the day, so I had time to run some errands, including grabbing the coffee and scones myself. Jade never actually agreed to get them, so I had to assume that meant she wouldn't.

After dropping off my dry cleaning and picking up some flowers for Jade's first official day, I headed to Joe Joe's Café for the rest of the treats. The flowers might have been a bit much, but I couldn't help myself. They were blue Forget Me Nots and reminded me of her eyes. I ordered a variety of scones because I wasn't sure what she would like, and I had four coffees, which I would give the extras to Scott and Tina, so it didn't look like everything I did was for her.

With all the goodies together, I realized I didn't have enough hands to bring everything in, so I texted Scott to help. As I grabbed the magazine with my dress in it, I heard a loud whistle.

"Look at you," Scott called out, and I had to hide my face so he wouldn't see me blushing.

I reached for the coffees and scones and hid inside the car as I responded. "What do you mean? I always dress like this." Once I felt like my face was no longer on fire, I turned around and handed him the bag and to-go container.

"Ms. Starr. Please. You can't bullshit a bullshitter. Who are you trying to impress?" He gave me a knowing look, but I didn't cave.

"We're not even in the building. You can call me Monica. And my only goal is to look good for myself."

That wasn't a lie. If I felt confident, it made me happier. I didn't care what everyone else thought. But it would secretly make my insides dance if Jade had the same reaction as him. However, I wouldn't give Scott the satisfaction of knowing that.

"Right. Mon-i-ca. You're peacocking. I don't care if you say it's for yourself or not. You're lying." If he had a free hand, I felt like he would've snapped his fingers in front of my face.

"Whatever. I'm wearing skinny jeans and a tank top. It's hardly worth noticing." I did put thought into my outfit today. I wanted something that hugged my slight curves and gave the appearance of casual but chic. I was going for looks good without trying, but apparently, I missed my mark. "Take the food and coffee inside while I get the flowers." I knew his mind would go crazy with that information, but I preemptively cut him off. "If you say anything else, you won't get to enjoy any of the goodies."

"I have no words." He shook his head as we walked toward the building.

When I made it inside, he followed me to my dressing room but kept his mouth shut.

Once we entered, he finally spoke. "May I?" He pointed toward the bag.

I gave him a warning look before agreeing.

"Thank you, Ms. Starr." As he laughed, he pulled out a chocolate chip scone, then grabbed a coffee. He took a large bite and, before chewing, followed it with a gulp of coffee. "Who are those flowers for?"

"I told you to zip it. My new stylist is coming today, and I wanted to make a good impression."

"Wait a minute. Since when?" He sounded rightfully skeptical.

I narrowed my eyes as I shook my head. "Haven't you heard? You catch more flies with honey, so I'm trying a new approach."

He shrugged as if he believed me. "That's cool. At least I reap the benefits of this new you." After taking another drink, he said, "Does she know what she's getting into?"

"What's that supposed to mean?"

Did he know it was her I'd dressed up for? Surely not. How could he? I'd known Scott for years, and he'd only seen me with men. He wouldn't jump to that conclusion. But if he did, then anyone could, and I couldn't have that. If people thought I was interested in her, my father would have a stroke, and I could kiss that regional job goodbye. I needed to cool my jets before things got out of hand.

"You fired three of your last assistants in six months. You're a lot to handle."

I still wasn't sure that was all he meant. The way he was staring at me felt like he was reading my every thought.

"None of that matters. They were incompetent. If she does her job, she will have nothing to worry about. Get the flowers and give them to her when she arrives."

"Why? I thought you were turning over a new leaf and trying to pick up flies or some shit. How would me giving her the flowers do that?"

"It doesn't matter. Just do it," I barked out.

"No. She'll think I'm hitting on her. Guys can't go around giving girls flowers. It's creepy."

Shit. What did that make me? I didn't even know if she was single, and I was dressing to impress and bringing in goodies. I was like Chad, making unwanted advances. No. I hadn't done anything yet. I'd get rid of the flowers and give the treats to the staff. I could fix this. Thank God Scott stopped me from making a huge mistake.

"You're right. That's not going to make things better. Take the stuff out of my room before she gets here."

"All of it?" He seemed confused.

"Yeah. Throw it away, give it away—I don't care. Go! She's due to arrive—"

"Hello?" Jade popped her head inside and eyed Scott with his arms full of the treats I'd bought. Then she turned to me. "I got scones and coffee, as you'd asked." She appeared perplexed, and I felt like an idiot.

"I'm sorry. I forgot I'd told Scott to bring them, too. Looks like we have double." I shrugged my shoulders in an "oh well" fashion, but I hoped she didn't think I was an airhead.

She finally came in as Scott scooted past her and closed the door. As she put down her bag and the stuff from Joe Joe's, I saw her outfit and knew I was in serious trouble. I'd never had someone set my pulse off like that from a look. She was a paradox and pulled me in like a magnet.

CHAPTER 9

Jade

PRESENT DAY

Monica was still entitled and thought everyone was her servant. I couldn't believe how stupid I was to think she had changed. Nothing about her was different—not even her looks. That wasn't true. Now she was better. She had filled out a little more, and a smile would escape every once in a while, which I never saw in high school. But that wasn't the point.

She'd played me for a fool. Actually, I played myself for a fool. I'd hung up on her, so she had no way of knowing I would do what she asked. She probably figured my action meant no, which it should have, but I thought she might reward me with a smile, and that was why I did it. Instead, *Scott* was the hero who came first, *and* he brought her flowers. I couldn't compete with that. I had no clue how to woo her.

I shook my head, trying to clear those thoughts floating around. I wouldn't go after a straight woman—especially not one who only cared about herself. Yeah, I had a thing for her in high school, but young me was stupid. She saw the outward appearance, and that was enough. But adult me knew there was so much more than looks. I needed depth, and Monica was a dried-up puddle. She wouldn't be able to stimulate my body *and* mind.

We were both standing, staring at each other, and I finally broke the ice. "Well, I guess it is my fault for not confirming. But, if I'm honest, this partnership won't work if you want to treat me like an employee. You said that you would work *with* me. I don't mind bringing you things *if* you ask *and* I have time. So, do you want to start over?"

After I finished my mini tirade, I took in her outfit, and she looked more gorgeous than usual. Her pants were so tight they looked like a second skin. And her little tank top had a scoop neck that hugged her body and showed the swell of her breasts. This was different from what I'd seen her in before.

In school, she always wore her cheerleading uniform on game days and usually some Catholic schoolgirl outfit on the other days. She was prim and proper. But today, nothing about what she wore said "prude." However, everything about it said, "I'm sexy AF, and I know it."

Her eyes were examining me like I was a map to a lost treasure, and she was searching for clues. I wasn't sure what we were doing ogling each other, but I liked it.

A smile spread across my face, and as her eyes came up, I licked my lips —slowly, letting my tongue bring my lower lip into my mouth on the way back.

"Fine." She had her ice shield back in place, and whatever had been happening was over.

"All right. What ideas did you have for your gown?" If she wanted to pretend nothing was going on, I would, too.

Without looking at me, she retrieved a magazine and tossed it in my lap. "Page 43. The dress Elizabeth Hurley wore. What do you think?"

I thought Elizabeth Hurley was beautiful, but Monica would blow her out of the water in that dress. I immediately thought back to all the times I'd sketched her, and my pulse was racing thinking about doing it again, only this time it would be with permission. Then my mind went back to the picture I'd drawn of her as Rose from the scene in *Titanic*, and my cheeks started to heat up.

"I think it would be perfect for you. It would fit your body type, and we could dress it up a little if you'd like. Maybe give it a train with a shorter hemline in the front? Or we could..." I pulled out my sketch pad and went to work.

She sat at the other end of the room, watching, but eventually came closer. By the time I was onto the bottom of the dress, she was right behind me, leaning over my shoulder, and I could feel her breath on my neck.

A little trickle of sweat beaded between my breasts, and I quickly wiped it away. Sitting up straight, I leaned back into her, and I could feel her heart pounding, but she didn't move. If I turned my head, our lips would be mere inches apart.

I swallowed hard and said, "Maybe something like that?"

She reached over my shoulder, picked up the pad, and swiftly stepped away from me. I missed the closeness and wondered if the moment felt as charged for her as it did for me.

She studied the drawing before walking back toward me. "This is great. But do you think maybe some sparkly see-through material should go into the open spots to make it more 'appropriate'?" She ran her hand over her chest and down her sides to accentuate her point, but I couldn't visualize anything except my hands caressing her.

"Um, yeah. This was merely a rough idea. I can put together various designs for you to choose from. Then we can go from there. You'll look stunning no matter what." I reached for the notepad, and if I didn't know better, I would think the compliment made her blush.

It looked like her cheeks had pinked a little, but I couldn't tell because she sat down in her chair and started fiddling with her makeup.

"Very well. I would appreciate it if you could lay out an outfit for me tonight." She was random with these robotic responses.

"Absolutely. What are your stories about tonight? I'll try to match the clothes with the tone."

Tilting her head to the side, she seemed confused. "No one has ever asked me that before. But I'll be interviewing two people from opposing sides of a bill lawmakers are trying to pass, and then there will also be a fluff piece about a dog rescuing a kitten from a storm drain. Thrilling stuff." She rolled her eyes, and I wondered if she enjoyed her job or just did it because the camera loved her.

Since it was a more businessy piece with the politics, what I had on would be perfect. We were about the same height and size, and I wondered if she would be okay with swapping outfits. It would put me on the map if she mentioned me on air. But it wasn't only about me. I honestly thought this jumpsuit would fit the mood. I'd bring it up and see what she thought. The worst she could do was veto it.

"What do you think about what I'm wearing?"

She glanced at me for a second, then continued putting on her makeup. I didn't know if she'd heard me or if she didn't think it required a response. When I thought she wouldn't say anything, I turned back to the racks to find something else.

"It's nice," she said so quietly I wasn't sure I'd heard her correctly.

I spun back around to face her. "Do you like it? If not, I'll move on."

"Move on? What does that mean?" She sounded defensive, which made no sense to me.

"To other choices? In my mind, I could see you wearing this for your interview. It's classy but with an edge. You could pull it off. But I'll find something else if you're not feeling it."

She stared at me in her mirror, and I couldn't tell what she was thinking.

"You want me to wear your clothes?" I could see her swallow hard. "That's absurd. What would you wear?" Her eyes narrowed, and I couldn't tell if she was mad or if that was her pensive expression.

"I mean, there's a whole rack of clothes here. I could throw something on and bring it back tomorrow or... I could wear yours. I don't care."

Her eyes scanned my entire body, and I figured she was silently critiquing me, but I was comfortable with who I was and how I looked. She probably wouldn't put me down to my face anyway. That was never her style. She would have one of her underlings do it. That made me wonder who her posse was now. Probably still fake people with their heads up their asses.

I didn't want to give her a chance to have a go at me, so I spoke up. "All right. We don't have much time, so..." I didn't even finish the thought because I was pretty sure my tone said stop fucking about.

"Fine. We'll both turn around so we can't see each other, and when you're done, toss the outfit on the table."

It wasn't like she didn't show me all of her before. Why was she suddenly being so modest? Oh well, I'd do as she asked because it would make my job a lot easier. As soon as she was dressed, I could hit the road. I'd told Iris that I might stop by after dinner.

I began taking off my clothes and quickly remembered I wasn't wearing a bra. Not that I needed one for my chest, but her tank top would cling to me, and it wouldn't be able to hide my excitement.

After placing my outfit on the table, I covered myself the best I could with my arm while I waited for her clothes. It was chilly in nothing but boyshorts, and I wondered what was taking her so long. I didn't want to ask her to hurry because I was afraid she would get angry, so I risked glancing over my shoulder, but she stood there in her bra and panties, not moving.

I was about to ask what was wrong, but we locked eyes when I looked in the mirror, and I couldn't avert my gaze. It appeared she couldn't either, as we stayed in this intense staring contest. I didn't understand what was happening, but my heart felt like it would beat out of my chest.

I finally broke free from the trance we were in, and my attention went to her chest. She was wearing a sheer bra that left little to the imagination. She didn't cover herself, so I risked turning around.

As I faced her backside, I removed my arm from my chest and saw her visibly gasp in the mirror. I might have misjudged the situation.

However, her expression didn't appear horrified but maybe intrigued. I wasn't sure what I was doing, but I stepped toward her.

Just then, there was a loud knock. "We need you on set in thirty minutes," someone yelled through the door, and I jumped back into the rack as if they were coming inside.

Things suddenly felt very awkward, and I wasn't sure if I could look at her again. "Um, could you put your clothes down so I can grab them?" I was thankful to be covered by a sea of dresses.

"They are there. Please put them on quickly because I may need your help with this outfit." She was business as usual, so maybe we could pretend nothing had happened.

Reaching my arm out of my hiding spot, I grabbed the clothes and brought them to me. The jeans were snug but not as tight as they were on her. She had better curves than I did. Once I had the tank top on, I stared at my chest to make sure I wasn't nipping out. Then I exited my refuge.

She was fully dressed, but I noticed she had the shirt buttoned to the neck, making her look like a stuffy librarian.

"Here. Let me help." I came up behind her and tied the straps.

She didn't say anything, and I was okay with that. There was no need to discuss the weird moment. We were better off moving past it since we would be working together.

After I finished with the straps, I moved in front of her and undid the top two buttons of her shirt, but it still didn't look right, so I continued with two more.

"What are you doing?" She swatted my hands away. "I can't wear it like that. My dad's a Judge, for fuck's sake. I have to represent him."

I wasn't aware there was a dress code for a Judge's daughter, but I wouldn't argue.

"Okay. Whatever you're comfortable with." I re-buttoned the last two, then fixed her collar. We were now gazing at each other, and her eyes darted to my mouth.

I'd seen that look before—it usually ended in a kiss, but I couldn't go there. Especially not after that charged moment we'd had. If I kissed her, I was pretty sure I wouldn't stop. And I was above letting lust control me. I had too many emotions right now, and they were clouding my judgment.

I gave her two pats on the shoulders and brushed her sleeves down. She might have been curious about things, but I couldn't open myself up to the hurt that would inevitably ensue when she realized her interest was fleeting.

To keep myself from doing something stupid, I took a step back. "That should do it. Do you need anything from me before I go?"

She stared at me for a second, then started walking away. "No. You're dismissed. Have a nice evening," she called over her shoulder as she headed back to her makeup station.

Dismissed? What did teenage me ever see in her? She could be vile. Here I was, thinking we were on the cusp of kissing, and she seemed completely detached. If I had given in to my thoughts, she probably would've gotten a restraining order against me.

I didn't need that drama in my life. My hormones needed to stay firmly in check from now on.

"Thank you, your majesty." I saluted her as I marched out the door. High school me was about to get her dreams crushed because there was no way I would ever go near Monica. She was a disaster waiting to happen.

CHAPTER 10

Monica

PRESENT DAY

Jade and I worked together all week, and I finally had a day off. I was thankful for the break because I had a lot going on inside my head. I needed to clear my mind, but I wasn't sure how to do that since I couldn't go back to Pilates. After that incident with Chad, it was no longer therapeutic for me—it was now weird.

I could always call Scott or my producer, Tina, but they would probably want to go out for drinks or something where there would be a lot of people, and I wasn't in the peopley mood. I could always distract my thoughts by watching TV.

After curling up on the couch and flipping through the stations, I didn't find anything worth my time, so I grabbed a book to get lost in. Maybe reading about someone else's drama could help me forget about my own.

There was some tension between Jade and me, and I didn't know how to fix it. Ever since that day we switched clothes, she had been short and snappy with me. I did my best not to engage in the snarkiness, but it was hard. I didn't understand where her hostility was coming from, and I wanted to keep the peace because even with her attitude, she was still the best stylist I'd ever had.

My phone rang, interrupting my internal dilemma. When I saw the caller ID and it was her, I almost didn't answer. I didn't want to ruin my day by getting into a fight with her. However, she might be angrier if I didn't pick up.

"Hello? Jade?"

"Hi. So, I finished those sketches, and I didn't know if you wanted me to drop them by." Her tone was deadpan and not at all friendly. But that was the most words she'd spoken to me consecutively in days—maybe this was a good sign.

"Sure. Do you want to go over—"

She cut me off. "I'll swing by your place and put them in your mailbox."

I guess it wasn't *that* good of a sign. She was still frosty, but I wanted to squash it all.

"Please come up. It would be better to go over the sketches with you. We have some great ideas when we work together. I'll order takeout?" I kept my voice light and inviting.

I could hear her shuffling stuff around in the background, but she didn't say anything.

"Jade. I'm not sure what I did, but we need to clear the air. If you come over, we can talk about it."

Finally, she stopped whatever it was she was doing. "All right. But if you say one thing that talks down to me, I'm done—with everything. The dress, work, all of it."

Talk down to her. I didn't do that. "Fine. When will you be here?"

"I just parked."

Shit. She was here? I was still in my PJs. Most people in their thirties probably didn't sleep until almost noon, like it was summer vacation, but I didn't think I would see anyone.

"Okay. Give me like five minutes? I, um, I just got out of the shower and need to get dressed."

Why did I lie? Did it matter if I'd slept in? She wasn't my mother. Oh well. It was too late to worry about it.

I quickly hung up the phone and rushed around like a maniac putting on my boobie prison and throwing on jeans and a T-shirt. As I brushed my teeth, the buzzer rang, and I let her up. Realizing I had no time to do anything with my hair, I swept it up into a messy bun and called it good.

I was walking back to the main area when there was a tap at the door. I opened it and saw Jade wearing a burned-out black T-shirt with black distressed skinny jeans and a pair of black high-top Nikes. It was like déjà vu hit me like a brick wall. Something about her felt eerily familiar, but she spoke, and it completely disappeared.

"Here are the drawings." She handed them to me as she walked inside.

I couldn't shake this feeling that I knew her from before, but that was impossible. There was something special about her, and I wouldn't have forgotten that.

"I'm sorry." I didn't want her to be hostile the entire time, and I hoped she could forgive me for whatever it was she was upset about.

"What are you sorry for?" She put her hand on her hip and cocked her head.

I didn't know I needed to be specific. Since I wasn't sure what I'd done, I thought a blanketed apology would work—I was wrong.

"For... being bossy?" I'd been told a time or twenty that I could be a touch on the authoritative side, but I didn't have time for people to screw things up. So it was better that I took control preemptively to avoid a crisis.

"That's the thing with you, *Monica*. You don't own up to your mistakes. Do you even know you make them?" She ran a hand through her hair, causing it to fall over her face.

I studied her for a second and was about to respond, but she wasn't done.

"When was the last time you said you were sorry for something and knew what you were apologizing for? Your words mean nothing because your actions speak so much louder." She wasn't holding back, and I felt like I'd had the wind knocked out of me.

I blinked a couple of times while I processed everything. Why did she say my name like that? It was like she thought I was a villain. But I was so far from that. If I did something wrong, I wanted to take responsibility. I hated how she saw me.

"Okay. I don't see how I could've made such a horrible mistake that has put you in Bitterville permanently but enlighten me. I need to know so that I can fix this. Jade, I promise you, I'm not a bad person." I wasn't someone who begged, but I would swallow my pride if I could show her I wasn't the wicked witch she thought I was.

"Right there. Put me in 'Bitterville.' Do you even hear yourself?"

I hung my head. There were better words to use than that.

"You're right. I didn't mean to sound harsh. I thought we were getting along, but you no longer wanted anything to do with me. You spent more of our time together listening to your earbuds than to me. And if I'm honest, it hurts."

That was more vulnerable than I intended, but somewhere in my head, I thought she and I were friends. But I didn't need friends, and she wanted nothing to do with me, so...

"I'm not trying to hurt you. But you need to see that the way you treat people isn't okay. You constantly talk down to us, making it seem like you think you're better than we are. It's like you don't see me but see through me. You've been this way forever."

Forever? That didn't seem like a word she could use since she'd known me for less than two weeks. And what did she mean I didn't *see* her? For a moment, I thought she knew how much I wanted to see of her, but I did a pretty good job of keeping those feelings under lock and key. Maybe I should be an actress.

"I see you, Jade. I see all of you. And I'm sorry if you think I have a superiority complex. But I'm worried that something will get missed or exposed if I don't stay on top of things. I can't risk that. My career is everything to me." I never thought I would be that person who put work before others, but it was the only thing in my life that I trusted. People would come and go and hurt me, but my job always made me happy.

She sighed. "I get that. Anxiety is all around. But it's the belittling that isn't acceptable. Telling people they're dismissed. Demanding instead of asking. It's these things that make you appear like a bitch. I know you're not used to someone questioning your authority, but when we started working together, it was with the idea that we were partners. But you repeatedly treat me like your employee. However, I'm my own boss. I have my own shop. And I don't need you to tell me what to do."

I didn't know that was how I came off. I thought being assertive was a good thing, but maybe somewhere along the line, I crossed into unfamiliar territory.

"Wow. I appreciate your honesty, and I can confidently say what I'm sorry for. I never meant to make you feel inferior because you are so much more than I could imagine. And I wasn't trying to be dismissive. I was going for business-like, but I must have missed the mark on that one."

"Being nice to someone isn't a weakness. It shows that you respect them, which goes a long way when working together. You get better productivity when someone feels safe and appreciated. Not when you try to rule over them."

"You get more flies with honey." I smiled, but my heart wasn't in it.

She stared at me and nodded. "Something like that."

This was the most challenging conversation I'd ever had, but it was also a wake-up call. I'd been going about life oblivious to the fact that my actions had been keeping people away. But I didn't want to do that with Jade. I wanted her to like me.

"Okay. I realize I messed up, but I'd like to make it right. Do you think we could have a do-over?" I hoped she could hear the sincerity in my voice, and I wanted to make my actions align with my words.

She shrugged, and I knew it would take a while for her to trust me, but I would put in the work.

"What if we can go over the drawings while we eat takeout and have a glass of wine? It can be a friendly day off work, and maybe we could even enjoy each other's company. What do you say?" I stared at her expectantly, and I could tell she was still hesitant.

It wasn't the first time I'd asked for a redo, so she was rightfully skeptical. I knew I tended to overcorrect when I was with her because I never wanted to cross a line from which I couldn't come back. But if I kept my feelings in check, maybe we could find that proper friend-coworker balance like I had with Scott and Tina.

"You're hard to stay mad at." She let a little smirk play across her face, and the fire inside me ignited.

Shit. I could feel my self-control leave my body, and now I would be making up with her—*alone*. I hoped I hadn't made a big mistake.

CHAPTER 11

Jade

PRESENT DAY

How many chances would I give this woman? What was that saying? Fool me once. Shame on you? She fooled me so many times that I might as well have had "idiot" stamped on my forehead.

But here she was, staring at me with those cobalt eyes, and I found myself nodding along, saying, "You're hard to stay mad at."

"Really? Cause you did a good job of it for days." I gave her a warning stare, and she held her hands up. "I'll stop there. What's your favorite food?"

At least she was reading the signs. Maybe my subtle hints could save her from herself.

"I like anything. Do you want to do Thai or Chinese?"

She scrunched up her face like she smelled something rotten.

"I'll take that as a, no?" I chuckled.

"I'm not that picky, but I don't like spicy, and Chinese is too salty. Oh, maybe we could do that French bistro? They have a seared tuna salad niçoise that is to die for."

"Do you hear how pretentious that sounds? Let's compromise. Shrimp tacos?" I'd never eaten French food, and I wasn't against it, but I thought she could use some flavor in her life.

"Tacos? I'm not a savage."

"No, you're a princess who drinks tea out of fine China," I said teasingly, but there was some truth to it.

"You think I'm that bad? I prefer to think I'm refined, but if you want tacos, then that's what we'll have. For the record, it will be my first."

I bit my lip so I wouldn't say something entirely inappropriate, but I couldn't keep the grin off my face.

"What? You think it's funny that I've never eaten a taco before?" She appeared confused, and I couldn't hold it in any longer as I laughed loudly.

"Why is that funny?" she demanded.

"It's not. I swear." Once I composed myself, I continued. "Do you want to get my favorite street tacos? They deliver."

"I'm not happy you're laughing at me, but I'll let it slide." She eyed me, and I kept my face neutral. "Well, I don't know anything about *street* food, so I'll leave it up to you. But I'm buying."

"Are you sure you don't want spicy? It might loosen you up a bit." I arched an eyebrow while pulling out my phone.

"No. It gives me heartburn. Do they have something sweet?"

"You want a sweet taco?" Was she doing this on purpose?

"I don't know. Is that an option? What are my choices?" She stared at me, and I could tell she was lost.

After bringing up the menu, I scooted closer for her to see. "There are burritos, quesadillas, fajitas, tacos. Pick your poison. Then we can narrow it down from there."

"What are you getting?"

"How about this? I'll order us a platter, and we can share. Is there anything besides spicy that you don't like?" I wanted her to enjoy the experience, but by the look on her face, she seemed nervous.

She shrugged. "I usually eat the same things, so I haven't tried much."

"Okay. Here's what I was thinking. Shrimp tacos topped with lettuce, tomatoes, sour cream, and mild salsa. And Pollo Mexicanas, which is a tortilla stuffed with chicken topped with guacamole and pico."

"That sounds interesting." Her expression changed, and it gave me hope.

"Yeah? So you want to give it a go?"

"All right. Let's do it." She smiled, and I placed the order.

She got plates and silverware out, and I set them on the table. "Is this a wine kind of meal? That's all I have to drink besides Perrier." She held a bottle of each in her hands.

Even her water choice was extravagant, but I wouldn't point it out again. It wasn't something she could change overnight.

"White wine pairs well with chicken, so I think that would be perfect."

"Look at you. Are you a connoisseur?" She sounded impressed, but I'd learned it from watching some *Housewives* episode.

"No. I'll drink anything with anything. I'm not picky."

"Hmm." She stared at me curiously while popping the cork off the bottle. "Tell me something about yourself?"

I pulled two glasses off her wine rack, and we both went to the table.

"I don't do well with open-ended questions." Since I didn't know where her head was, I felt uncomfortable spilling random facts about myself.

"Okay. What do you like to do in your free time?" She poured us each a glass, then relaxed as she waited for my answer.

I scoffed. "Is that a thing? Having your own business might seem like you can make your own hours, but I want to start a clothing line so I don't get downtime." I had a ton of things I needed to catch up on, but for some reason, being here felt right.

"But what would it be if you did have time to do anything you wanted?" She seemed hung up on this question, but my mind immediately went to a no-go zone as I watched her wipe a drip of wine off the glass, then suck it off her finger.

If I could do anything right now, it would be to throw her on the table and eat her for lunch, but I couldn't say that. My face was getting hot, so I took a big gulp. The crisp sweetness tickled my throat but cooled me down.

Once I got my thoughts in order, I gave my G-rated version. "I enjoy many things. Music, drawing, museums, plays, ballet. Anything dealing with the arts. What about you?"

"I spend most of my free time alone. I feel like I have to be 'on,' so when I get to unwind, I prefer to do it without the pressure of others judging."

That was deeper than I thought. I figured she would say she enjoyed jet-setting to exotic places and hobnobbing with famous people. She seemed like the type who would name-drop. As the thought left my head, I realized I was one of those people she was trying to break away from. Maybe her persona was to be frigid because she didn't think she could be herself. That made me sad.

"Do you feel like your life is under a microscope?" I couldn't imagine being in the public eye. That would make me want to crawl under a rock to get some privacy, too.

"I never thought of it like that, but I guess so." She stared at her glass while she swirled her wine around. "My dad is a Judge, and my brother, Spencer, and I have certain expectations placed on us. He followed in my father's footsteps and is a lawyer heading toward a judgeship. I was supposed to be a doctor, but that wasn't my calling. My one act of rebellion was to go into broadcasting." A wistful expression crossed her face, and I couldn't imagine what it would have been like for her to have everything planned out.

69

"So, your parents weren't happy to have a daughter on the news?" I quirked a brow. It seemed like that would be something to be proud of.

"Oh, I don't know about that. They have gotten over it for the most part. But I always hear how great my brother is. He has a wife and kids, and I'm not even dating anyone." She scoffed, and it sounded like she was resentful, but I didn't know of what.

"I guess I'm sensitive right now. I spoke to my mother earlier, and she gushed about my ex, Damon, and his wife and children. Then she proclaimed I was too old to have children on my own and should look into surrogacy." She took a big drink, and her glass was now empty.

Her life didn't sound as charmed as it appeared from the outside. I felt a pang of regret for thinking she lived on easy street. It just went to show that we all have issues, but those didn't excuse poor behavior. However, her mother sounded like a piece of work. It helped me understand her and maybe to be slightly more tolerant.

Another interesting tidbit she dropped was how Damon was a husband and father. I smiled because I imagined that suited him. He was always sympathetic to me, so I could imagine how good he would be with his family.

I watched as she poured herself some more and then twisted the stem in her fingers. "The funny thing is that I don't want kids. So I wouldn't say I missed any boats. If anything, I dodged a bullet." After taking another swig, she set her glass down, and I slid it back from the edge.

"Why don't you want kids?" Not that it mattered, but I was curious.

"I thought I was asking the questions." She had a touch of a slur, and I wasn't surprised. She had chugged almost a fourth of the bottle in one gulp.

"By all means. This is your interview," I joked.

Before she could get another question out, the food arrived. She went to stand, but I waved her off. I wasn't sure how tipsy she was, so I buzzed them in.

When I brought the food back, the smells of chili powder and cilantro wafted in the air.

"Oh my God. That looks delicious." She stared at the tacos and licked her lips.

I divvied out our plates and grabbed a Perrier for each of us. It was prudent not to drink all of the wine right now. We needed to pace ourselves.

We were ready to eat, and I wanted to memorialize this event since she was a taco virgin. Before she took her first bite, she picked up a knife and a fork.

I reached out my hand, stopping her before she broke the shell to pieces. "What are you doing? You can't eat that with a fork."

She looked at me like I had gone mad. "Watch me." Using the fork and knife, she shattered the shell entirely and stared at the ruined taco. "What am I supposed to do with it now?"

I laughed at how serious her question was, but I'd warned her. She was like a defiant child.

"I guess eat it with a spoon?" It wasn't Humpty Dumpty.

"How are you going to eat yours?" She appeared perplexed.

"Like every other person in the world—with my fingers." I picked up my taco, took a bite, and then carefully put it back on my plate. After swallowing, I said, "Ta-da."

"You're like an animal. My mother wouldn't allow you at the table if you ate with your hands. I'll get a spoon and scoop mine like someone civilized."

I watched her walk into the kitchen, and she seemed so relaxed that I couldn't help but smile. Where was this side of her all those years ago? Maybe she and I could have been friends.

"All right. But I want to see your face when you take your first bite." I studied her, and she appeared embarrassed.

"No. You aren't going to watch me eat. That's weird." She sat back down.

"Come on. It's your first one. I want to know if you like it, and your expression will tell me so much more than your words."

She rolled her eyes but agreed. "Fine. One bite, then you have to turn away. This looks messy, and I don't want to make a fool of myself."

"I think we're past that, yeah?" I chuckled.

"What? I had no idea the shell would do that. You bit into it, and it didn't break." She countered, and she had a point.

However, I'd told her it was a bad idea, but she was too stubborn to care.

"Touché. But go ahead. Take in all the flavors. It will make your taste buds dance." I stared as she started spooning up all the ingredients.

Then she popped it into her mouth. She chewed slowly, closing her eyes as if she were savoring the flavor. After she swallowed, she dabbed the corner of her lips with a napkin, and a look of contentment crossed her face. She even let a small "hmm" escape.

"You like it?" I beamed, and she stared at me, but then her gaze darted to my lips.

That almost imperceptible action unleashed all the thoughts I'd been pushing away, and all I could think about was my desire for her.

Maybe it was the wine talking or that she'd opened up to me, but I wanted to lower this wall and let her in.

CHAPTER 12

Monica

PRESENT DAY

This was my first taco ever, and Jade was right. It was a flavor burst. The shrimp was grilled and seasoned perfectly. The texture of the shell was crunchy but mixed with the smoothness of the sour cream, gave it a wonderful mouthfeel. As I took it all in, Jade watched with the brightest smile, and I could feel myself slipping under her spell.

Her baby blues were drawing me in, but it was her lips that held my gaze. I couldn't stop staring as her tongue slowly slipped out of her mouth. There was something so sensual about the gesture, and I wanted to know how she tasted.

An image of her tongue caressing mine popped into my head, and my heart felt like it was running a marathon in my rib cage. Before my mind could control my body, I was out of my chair, standing over Jade. Looking down at her, I realized I didn't know what I was doing and hoped she would decide the next move.

She must have been a mind reader because she placed her hands on my hips and pulled me onto her lap. I couldn't believe I was straddling her as her fingers caressed my back. My breathing picked up, but I never broke eye contact. It was like some intense foreplay. When her hands made their way to my head, she released my bun, setting my wild hair free.

"You are so fucking gorgeous," she purred, and my insides turned to jelly. Her chest was moving up and down almost frantically, and I could feel her shaking under me.

There was no way she was as nervous as I was. She was so confident, but there was something vulnerable in her eyes.

She swallowed hard and bit her lower lip. "I've imagined this moment a million times. Are you sure this is okay?"

My God. She must have thought about me every second of the day. Surprisingly, that only made me want her more.

"Yes," I said with more bravado than I was feeling. But I didn't want her to stop because she thought I was scared.

Without saying another word, she brought my head down until our mouths collided in an exciting but terrifying way. I'd never felt anything like this. Her lips were soft and supple and molded to mine perfectly. There was no facial hair scratching my skin. Everything was smooth, and when her tongue touched the seam of my lips, I opened willingly, hoping she would give me more. I *needed* more.

I moaned as she massaged my tongue with hers ever so gently. While cradling my head like I was her most prized possession. I felt like I was floating yet falling, and I didn't want this to end. The only problem was that our position wasn't all that comfortable. I wondered if she wanted to take this to my bed or at least the couch, but I wasn't sure if she thought that meant we'd have sex. I'd never slept with anyone I'd just met, but I felt so safe with her like I'd known her my entire life.

I broke the kiss but kept my lips on hers. "Do you want to take this to my room?" I couldn't believe I'd asked a near stranger that, but I would have kicked myself if I hadn't. That kiss awakened something inside me, and I wanted to explore more.

"Are you sure?" She was massaging my head. Then gently trailed her fingers down my body until settling on my hips. "Mon, we can go as slow as you want. I'm in no hurry."

Mon? No one had called me that in ages, but I liked the nickname coming out of her mouth. It made me feel special, and it only reinforced the urgency inside of me.

"I want this. So bad." I pulled back so I could gaze into her eyes again. "You do things to me that no one ever has. There's this throbbing between my legs that's begging for release." Fuck. That got a little too real and slightly desperate, but she seemed to like it.

She let out a low, guttural sound as she urged me to stand. I reached out to her, but she didn't grab my hand.

"What's wrong?" Something shifted, and she no longer had that hunger in her eyes.

"I think we should finish eating and then go over the sketches like we had planned." She turned back to the table and didn't look at me.

What the hell? I thought she was into me. She was the one who pulled me onto her lap. Now she was going to finish lunch as if nothing had happened. Fuck that.

"You know what? I'm not feeling so well. I'll look over the designs later. You should go." I felt so stupid.

How could I have let myself give in like that? What would happen if she told people? I inhaled deeply and released it slowly.

"What do I have to give you to keep this between us?" I couldn't read her expression, but she appeared sad. Although maybe that was me projecting my own feelings.

"Monica. I'm not going to tell anyone anything. It's no one's business, but please don't shut me out. I wasn't turning you down." She stood up and put her hands on my cheeks, and her ocean eyes locked on mine. "I just don't want you to be under the influence the first time we..." She scanned my body, and I could see her chest rising faster.

"I'm not drunk. I want this." I pointed back and forth between us. "I want you." Now I sounded pathetic, like I was begging, but this wasn't something I just wanted—it was something I *needed*.

She made another growling sound. "And I want you, too. More than you could know. But the only thing I want to be intoxicating is me."

"But if not now, then when?" I was afraid that if I didn't give in to my desires tonight, I might not have the courage to do it later.

"You want to put it in your calendar?" She laughed as she brushed my hair away from my face. "If you want me to take you on a date and set the mood for a night of seduction, I'll do it."

A date? What was she talking about? "We can't."

"Can't what?" She tilted her head in confusion.

"We can't go on a date. If word got out, my dad would have a stroke." My heart was racing again, but this time it was from panic, not anticipation. "I like you, Jade. A lot. I think you're funny and smart and confident, and you stand up for yourself. You're everything I wish I could be. But I don't have the luxury of being open with my life. Everyone loves a good scandal, but I can't be the story. I report the news, not make it."

"Why did I think you were different?" Her eyes glossed over, and it was like she was no longer present. "Your secret's safe with me, but I'm done. How I ever thought you could change was beyond me."

She walked toward the door, and I wanted to call out for her to stay, but I couldn't even process what had happened.

CHAPTER 13

Jade

HIGH SCHOOL

The more I sketched Monica, the more infatuated I became with her. She was like a drug to me, and I wasn't even sure why. She was gorgeous, which pulled me in, but in my head, she was more. Sometimes I wondered if I liked her or the idea of her. I had built up this amazing person in my head, and I worried the reality wasn't as good as the fantasy.

I was mesmerized as I watched her practice some of her cheers. She was the team captain and performed each stunt flawlessly, but she didn't appear excited to be there. Maybe she saved her enthusiasm for the actual games. I didn't know because I'd never seen her in action before.

Sporting events weren't my bag. They seemed boring, but maybe that was because I didn't understand the rules most of the time. But since my mom couldn't pick me up until four today, I caught a glimpse of what I was missing. Well, at least the part I would want to see anyway.

I sat on the bleachers, pretending to do my homework, but I couldn't take my eyes off her. She commanded the attention of everyone, including me. I felt a bump on my shoulder, pulling me out of my daze. When I looked over, I saw Damon. They had a game tonight, so he must not have had practice.

He flashed that boyish smile, and I was confused about why he was here. "Hey. You need a ride?"

"Oh, no. My mom is coming to get me. I was doing some homework while I waited."

"That's cool. Um, are you going to the game tonight? I could use the support." He winked, and the gesture made me feel weird.

Sometimes I almost thought he was flirting with me, but that was ridiculous as he had the hottest girl in school, and I was nothing like her.

"No. I don't get sports." I shrugged my shoulders.

"I could tutor you." He sat down next to me.

"Thanks. But I think I'm okay being in the dark about that. It's too competitive."

"It can be, but we're good, so we are the competition." His dimples popped, and I couldn't help but smile, too. "If you won't go to the game, do you think you'll go to the after party?"

I laughed nervously. "Noooo. I don't do parties. If you haven't noticed, I'm not exactly popular, and I don't get invited." I realized how pathetic that sounded, but it was true. "Not that I want to be invited. Because Tara would be there, and she would make it hell." I hoped he wasn't thinking I was fishing for him to ask me.

"Don't worry about Tara. I'll handle her. Why don't you come tonight? I'm sure I could swing by and pick you up after the game." He brushed his hair to the side, out of his eyes, and stared at me. "It could be fun. There will be drinking and dancing." He did this little shoulder shake, and my smile grew. "I can see it on your face that you want to come."

I looked out at the field and watched as Monica did three backflips and ended with a twist. She took my breath away.

Damon must have realized that I was staring at her because he said, "They're talented. If you go to the game, you could watch them do an entire show at halftime."

Did he know I was ogling Monica? Oh my God, would he tell her?

I needed to play this off so as not to make things awkward. "Oh, I don't need to see more, but they are impressive. I could never do anything that took that much coordination."

"I'm sure you're impressive in your own right. But practice is almost over, and I am giving Monica a ride home. Why don't you write your number, and I'll call you after the game to see if you're up for the party?" He pointed to my sketchpad.

I glanced toward Monica and saw her watching us, but she seemed confused, not angry. "Okay. But don't count on it."

He stuffed the paper in his pocket. "I'm pretty persuasive." He gave me a finger gun as he took off toward Monica.

I couldn't hear what they were saying, but he immediately laced his fingers through hers and walked off.

My mom arrived fifteen minutes later, and I got in the car.

"Hey, honey. How was school today?" She leaned in and kissed me on the cheek.

I was glad no one was around to see it, but it made me feel good nonetheless. My mom was very nurturing and always encouraged me to be kind and loving toward others. Granted, she didn't know how badly I was picked on at school. It was something that I always kept in the back of my mind.

"It was good. I might even go out tonight." I knew that would make her happy because she always wanted me to be social like her.

"Oh? Is there someone special that you're going with?" She glanced at me, then brought her eyes back on the road.

"No! It's just a friend."

We'd never talked about my sexuality, but I knew my mom wouldn't care, as she was a free spirit and had dated women before. But I was too shy to tell her about any crushes. Not that I had a lot of them. Only one —Monica.

"Okay. I won't push, but I'm happy that you're going to do something. It will be good for you."

When we got home, I did my chores around the house and then jumped in the shower before dinner. I dressed as if I was going tonight, but I still wasn't sold. The thought of putting myself out there scared the hell out of me. But it was an excuse to see Monica outside school, which trumped my fear.

After we ate, I started a new drawing and waited. I wasn't sure how long the game would take, so I kept myself occupied to pass the time. A little after nine, the phone rang. I rushed to answer it but stopped myself. I didn't want him to think I was waiting around for his call. So before I picked up, I let it ring twice for good measure.

"Hello?" I kept my voice neutral.

"Is Misty there?"

"This is she. Who is this?" I knew it was Damon because he was the only person who called me that, but I didn't want to come off overeager.

"Hey. It's Damon. So, we won the game tonight, and the party will be sweet. You wanna come?" The enthusiasm in his voice got me excited.

"Congratulations. That's great."

"Damon, let's bounce. Come on, man." I heard in the background, but I had no idea who had said it.

"Sorry, we're heading out. What's your address? I'll swing by." He must have been confident I was going since I hadn't committed, but he was right.

I smiled at the thought. "1978 Cherry Hill Drive."

"Aiight. Can't wait to see you. It's going to be fire." He hung up, and I questioned what I'd gotten myself into.

He sounded like a completely different person, and I wondered if everyone was. I didn't fit in with the people at school. Would they be more sociable in a relaxed setting, or was I setting myself up for more severe torture because there were no rules? Maybe I should cancel?

"Hey, sweetie. Who was that?" My mom's inquiry stopped me from continuing down the spiral I was on.

"It was Damon. A boy from school. He's the one who asked me to the party."

She squealed with delight, and I didn't have the heart to tell her I'd changed my mind. "I'm so happy you are doing something with *friends*. I hope you have so much fun! And don't do anything I would do." She laughed as she pulled me into a bear hug.

"Thanks, Mom. What time do I need to be home?" Hopefully, she would give me an early curfew, and I wouldn't feel bad about not staying long.

"You're eighteen. I trust your judgment." She released me from her embrace but kept her hands on my shoulders. "But I want you to be safe —no drinking and driving. No getting into a car with someone under the influence of any kind. And you know you can call me anytime if you need a ride."

I was so lucky to have her as my parent. My dad left when I was a baby, but I never felt like I was missing something because she always made me feel like I was the most important person in the world.

I threw my arms around her one more time. "I love you."

"You're the best, and I love you, too, sweetheart. Please enjoy yourself."

A few minutes later, Damon honked his horn, and I was glad he didn't come in. I didn't want my mom to think there was more to this than it was.

"Bye, Mom. See you soon."

"Not too soon! Be safe and have fun!"

I rushed out to his truck, hoping to sit next to Monica, but it was just the two of us this time, which made me sad. But surely I would see her at the party.

"Hey, thanks for picking me up. And congratulations again."

"Of course. I'm glad you decided to come. And thanks. It was a comeback victory, so it made it even more special." He squeezed my knee before taking off.

Dance music was on in the background, and I found myself nodding along to the beat.

"You like to dance?" He glanced at me from the corner of his eye.

"No. Remember? Coordination? I don't have that." I chuckled.

"We'll see. I bet you'll be out there tearing up the dance floor after a drink or two."

"I don't drink."

"That's cool. Are you straight edge?" he questioned but didn't seem put off if I was.

"No. I just like to be aware." I was picked on enough. If I did something stupid under the influence, I would never live it down.

"Fair enough. We're here, but maybe you should stay close to me until you feel comfortable." He shut off the engine but didn't get out.

"Thank you. I appreciate that."

"Of course." He stared into my eyes and licked his lips, but someone hit the driver's side window, drawing our attention.

"We won! Can you fucking believe it? You're like a hero." The guy jumped up and down, shaking the truck bed.

"Knock it off, Paul. You're going to tear up my shocks." He shook his head and opened his door.

I was thankful for the disruption because sometimes, the moments with Damon felt slightly intense. We both got out, and he immediately came to me and whispered.

"You okay?"

The music was blaring, and we weren't even inside yet.

"Yeah. Where's Monica?" I didn't want her to know I came with Damon without her.

"I don't know. She and I broke up."

I could have been pushed over with a feather. I was so stunned. "When? I saw you with her after school."

"I know. It was before the game. I think we make better friends, and she agreed. It wasn't nasty or anything." He reached out his hand, and I took it, but then I worried that this was a more-than-friends outing in his mind.

As we entered the house, some guy shoved a beer in Damon's hand, and "Low" was pumping through the speakers. I searched the room to see if there was anyone I was friendly with but came up empty. Damon let go of me to open the can, and someone smacked into my shoulder, causing me to fall into him, knocking his beer to the floor. We both jumped back so we didn't get splattered.

"I'm so sorry." I covered my mouth with my hands, and he gave an easy smile.

"No worries. None got on me, and it's cheap beer. Are you okay?"

The pungent smell floated through the air, and I stared at the mess I had caused. Damon took my elbow and guided me away from it.

"Do you think we should get something to clean it up?" I questioned once we made our way to the kitchen.

It was right in the middle of the entryway, and I would hate if someone slipped on it.

"Nah. It'll be fine." He strolled over to the cooler and pulled out a cold one. "Can I get you anything? It looks like there is soda for mixers over there." He pointed to a table covered with cheap liquor.

"I'm okay. Thanks." While I waited for him to decide what to do next, Monica and her flock entered. I locked eyes with her, and she gave an almost imperceptible smile.

"Everytime We Touch," by Cascada, came on, and I felt like everyone had disappeared, and it was just Monica and me. The way she never stopped looking at me made me wonder if she felt the same. But before I could get lost in her, a screeching voice broke the spell.

"What are you doing here, freak?" Tara called out, and I turned my head to see that she was talking to me.

I watched as she marched over, but I couldn't respond because my mouth felt as dry as sandpaper. This was what I was afraid of. Disdain radiated off her, and it was directed at me.

"No one invited you." She reared back, and before I knew what hit me, a drink was dripping off my face.

"Seriously, Tara? What the fuck is wrong with you? Why are you such a bitch?" Damon rushed to my side and took off his shirt to dry me.

"I can't believe you, Damon. Did you bring her?" Tara spat out.

"It's none of your business, but yes. She's with me. Now back off." His voice was protective, making me feel a little safer, not that I thought much worse could happen.

After I wiped my face, I saw Monica staring at me with what appeared to be concern. But when she locked eyes with Tara, her expression changed. I wondered if she would say something, but Tara cut in.

"Can you believe this?" she asked the flock of sheep. "Mistake is here with Damon just hours after he and Mon broke up. If you ask me, she deserved worse than a drink in her face." She cackled, and I looked at Monica.

She wasn't smiling, but she wasn't defending me, either. Instead, she nodded as if she agreed. What the fuck was she doing? A moment ago, she seemed sympathetic, but now it was like she was giving Tara the green light.

"You're a skank, and you'll never belong here. Damon is only after you because you're a virgin, and he thinks you're desperate to give it up." Tara was pleased with herself, and I wanted to cry, but I refused to give them the satisfaction.

"I'm going home," I told Damon, and he shook his head.

"No. None of that is true." He held my hand, but I pulled away. Then he turned and shouted, "Tara, get the fuck away from us! You have no idea what you're talking about."

"Keep telling yourself that, baby boy. You better watch her. It looks like the home-wrecker's gonna cry." She rubbed her fists under her eyes like she was wiping tears, and everyone laughed.

Monica mouthed what appeared to be "sorry," but it didn't matter because her actions spoke way louder than anything she could have said. I handed Damon his shirt back, and I headed toward the door.

I couldn't even look back to see if Monica was laughing, too, because she'd already broken my heart enough for a lifetime.

CHAPTER 14

Monica

PRESENT DAY

I didn't understand what happened last night and how things went so horribly wrong. And what did she mean by, "How I ever thought you could change was beyond me"? We barely knew each other, but she already had an opinion about me, which didn't appear good.

I wasn't sure what to say or if I should forget everything. However, that would be hard for me because no one had ever kissed me like that, and I didn't want it to be the last time. I wished she understood I couldn't have a public romance because of my job and family. Not just with a woman but with anyone.

She acted like me wanting privacy made me a bad person. I didn't owe anyone my life story. No one did. I never asked her for hers. I guess my only option was to let her set the tone for our relationship going forward, but if I was honest, I already missed her. I had dated two people long-term, and I never cared whether they were around. In fact, I preferred when they weren't so that I could breathe.

But I had one not-even-a-date with Jade, and I missed her company—her intense looks. She made me feel like I was the only person in the room. Even if a supermodel walked by, I didn't think her eyes would drift. She saw other sides of me and called me on my bullshit, which, for some reason, I found attractive. It made me realize I needed someone who challenged me.

The more I thought about her, the more I could feel myself slipping into a pity party. I needed to get out of my head, so I looked through the designs she'd left. After flipping through a few, I found the perfect one.

Jade wasn't just a stylist. She was an artist. The intricate detail she put into these drawings was incredible. She even drew me wearing the dress. I hoped I looked as good in real life as in her sketch. I wished she was here so I could tell her how amazing she was, but I would have to wait until I saw her tomorrow.

I placed all her pictures in my bag and couldn't help but feel anxious. I didn't know how she would respond to me, but I hoped she wouldn't go back to giving me the cold shoulder. Because if she didn't look at me the same, it would break my heart.

I had a fitful night of sleep because my mind was heavy with worries. I couldn't make any grand gestures to make up with Jade because I didn't want anyone to know how I felt about her. But at the same time, I wasn't sure I could go on if I didn't have her on my side. I was in a lose-lose situation... Unless, over this time apart, she developed an understanding of my actions and was okay with them.

It was now three o'clock, and I was ready for work. I drove in a little early because I wanted to talk to Scott. He always made me feel better when I was down, and I was about as low as I could go. Jade had the upper hand, and I would have to go along with whatever she decided.

When I pulled into the garage, I called Scott to have him meet me. I didn't want to speak about anything private inside the building—the walls had ears.

He climbed into the passenger seat and stretched his long legs. "What's up? I took my break early. Are you okay?"

"Oh. Yeah. I'm fine. Great, really." My tone sounded fake to me.

He studied me as he tilted his head from side to side. "Then why did you 9-1-1 me to the garage?"

"I suppose that was a bit hasty. I thought we could chat out here, where it's quiet."

His eyes narrowed. "Okay. About what?"

"How's softball going?" I wasn't even sure he started playing this year yet.

"You tell me there's an emergency, and you want to know about softball?" Now he sounded annoyed.

"I need to take my mind off some things, and I thought talking to you would help." I gave him my "damsel in distress" look.

"All right. What things?"

I let out a heavy sigh. "If I tell you something, do you promise to withhold judgment?"

"When have I ever judged you? When have you ever done anything worth being judged for?" He laughed, and I slapped his arm. "Hey. Don't assault an officer."

"Whatever. So this weekend. I kissed someone. And not just a kiss, but... A. *Kiss*."

He nudged me with his elbow. "Then what happened?" His interest was piqued now.

"Nothing. We got into an argument, and it all went tits up before it could lead to more."

"Monica, I know you don't understand how dates work since you never go on them, but you win some, and you lose some. It's no big deal."

"But I like them and don't want it to be over." I hated how desperate I sounded.

He stroked his chin as if he had a beard. "What was the argument about? Is it something unforgivable?"

I didn't even understand, so how could I explain it? "I guess they were upset because I said I didn't want a public relationship." At least, that was my takeaway from her reaction.

"So, you wanted a booty call, and they said no? Who is this dude? I need to smack some sense into him. Does he know who you are? You're not someone who gets rejected."

He saw me like everyone else did—entitled. That wasn't me, and I needed to prove that to Jade. I was a good person, but I had expectations set for me, and there was nothing I could do about them. I wasn't trying to make her feel like a one-off. But I needed discretion in all aspects of my life.

"Stop it. I didn't say I wanted casual sex." I rubbed my temple because I felt a headache coming on. "But you know how it is. If someone gets wind of who I'm dating, both of our lives will be plastered all over various media outlets. I don't need that pressure. And I don't want to put that on them either."

"Okay. But once you started to get serious, then you'd go public, right?"

That wasn't an option, but I couldn't very well explain why without outing myself to him. "I don't know why it is anyone's business who I'm seeing. Why would that matter?"

He turned toward me and clasped his hands together. "I'm going to break this down for you. Your boy is proud of you. He wants to show you off. Take you to dinner. Go on vacations. If no one knows about you two, how would that work?" He raised his bushy eyebrows at me.

"It's okay to stay under the radar, but they have to know they're a priority. And if you want to hide them away, they'll only feel like a dirty secret, which isn't how you want a relationship to be. Amirite?" He rested his hand on my shoulder, but it didn't offer me much comfort.

My choices were to lose the first person who set my world on fire or lose my dream job and probably my family. I wasn't okay with either of those, but I suppose I would have to choose.

"Thanks, Scott. You've given me a lot to think about. We can go inside now. But please don't mention this to anyone?"

"I got you. Come on." He winked, and we exited the car.

As we walked to the building, I heard a noise behind us, and we both turned around.

"Hey, Ms. Miller. How are you?" Scott stopped and waited for her, so I felt obligated to do the same.

"I'm well. Thank you for asking." She smiled at him but didn't even glance my way.

I wouldn't have this. I thought I would let her take the lead, but her lead sucked.

"Hey, Jade. I liked all of your drawings, but I think I know which one I want you to make. I brought them with me." I patted my bag and gave her my best smile.

"Excellent." She still didn't make eye contact and kept walking. "You can give it to me when we get inside."

If Scott noticed her coldness toward me, he didn't let on.

"Ooo. I'm excited to see this." He rubbed his hands together. "Wait a minute. I do get to see this, right?"

"You want me to wear it around the studio?" I asked disbelievingly.

"Or you could not be a smart ass and take a picture." He laughed.

"That seems doable." I gave him a shy smile and leaned in so Jade couldn't hear. "And thank you."

"No problem, Ms. Starr," he whispered. "Have a nice evening, you two." He said boisterously.

"Thank you. I wish the same for you," Jade responded, and I blew him a kiss.

Even though Scott could be a little ornery, I knew he would always have my back, and I was grateful for his friendship.

Jade and I left him at his stand and made our way to my dressing room. When we got inside, I shut the door and turned to her.

I realized I again owed her an apology, but I wasn't sure if she would forgive me. "I'm sorry." I took a deep breath. "I never meant to make you feel like a dirty secret."

Her jaw clenched, but she didn't say anything. Her eyes were like ice, but I hoped they would soften if I continued.

"I felt something with you. Not just from that life-altering kiss, but before that." My only chance to make this right was to pour my heart out and hope that she could see my sincerity.

"The first time you touched me while taking my measurements, there was a spark. That sounds crazy, but it's true. I never in my life felt like I needed someone else around. I usually find people to be draining. Even people I thought I loved." I paused, gauging her reaction, and she seemed to be softening, so I continued.

"But with you, I feel charged—alive. You don't take any shit from me. You make me see things differently—especially myself. There's this weird sense of familiarity about you that makes me comfortable and relaxed. I know you have no reason to give me a chance. I can't give you a traditional relationship, but I would kick myself if I didn't at least let you know how I felt about you."

She stood there, unmoving, with an intensity in her eyes. But I couldn't tell if the look meant "I forgive you" or "fuck you."

When she didn't respond, I assumed my words didn't matter to her. She had made it clear before that it was actions that meant something. So, if I wanted her to know how I felt, I had to show her. I moved in closer until her back hit the door. Now I had her caged in. I locked eyes with her, silently asking if she wanted me to stop.

She never flinched as we stood in this staring contest, so I closed the distance, crashing my mouth against hers. She tasted like cherries, and I wanted to deepen the kiss. But before I could make another move, she spun me around, switching our positions.

With her thigh pressed firmly between my legs, she took my lower lip into her mouth and sucked on it. Then she did that sexy growly thing as her hands reached under the hem of my shirt.

Her fingers were icy yet set me on fire. My breathing picked up as her lips moved to my neck. I could feel my nipples harden and a throbbing between my legs. She had ignited something inside of me that could no longer be contained.

My whole life, I thought I was broken because everyone spoke of desire, but it was something I'd never felt... until now. I craved her attention— her gaze, her touch, her breath. I wanted it all. I needed every part of her to cover my body, and if I didn't get it, I might scream in frustration.

It was as if she was reading my thoughts because she was on the move. Sliding her hands under my shirt, she pushed my bra out of the way and cupped my breasts. The sensation shot straight to my core and left a pool in my center. I was afraid my knees would give out, but she pressed me against the door, ensuring I wouldn't fall.

How had I never experienced this feeling? She locked eyes with me, and in that moment, I'd never felt so safe but vulnerable. And I knew right then that she could break my heart. I needed to proceed cautiously, but I was powerless against her touch.

CHAPTER 15

Jade

PRESENT DAY

I couldn't believe Monica's words, but more so, her kiss. I knew she wasn't in a spot to be pursued. At least not by me. But my body responded faster than my brain, and I couldn't stop. She was clear-headed when she spoke to me, which was all the permission I needed to unleash this desire I'd had for her.

My hands and lips roamed her body, and all I could think about was finishing what we had started the other night. The problem was, I'd dreamed of this moment for years, and there was no way I would rush it. I couldn't have sex with her up against her dressing room door. Anyone could walk in, which would ruin our chance of being together again.

I needed to slow things down before we reached the point of no return. As I stared into her darkened eyes, I tried to even my breathing. I moved my hands from her breasts to her hips and watched as her tongue wetted her lips. That simple gesture had me aching to taste her again.

"You have no idea what you do to me." I pressed my forehead to hers and brought my hands up to cup her face.

"Is it anything like what you do to me?" She grabbed one of my hands and placed it on her rapid heart.

"Yeah. It's like that." I put her other hand on my chest so she could feel it, too.

Standing there, face-to-face, with our hearts thundering around, it was apparent we were both charged, but my logical mind kicked in.

"I'm going to take a step back." As I went to move, she held on to me, keeping me close.

"Please don't." Her tone was pleading, and I wasn't sure what she wanted, but I stayed there.

"Monica. I know we're attracted to each other, but you know we can't be together. You already said that. So what are we doing?"

"No." She shook her head but kept eye contact with me. "I said we couldn't have a traditional relationship, but I *want* to be with you." She now wrapped her arms around my neck and pulled me in, pressing her lips softly but urgently against mine, and I couldn't help but kiss her back.

As I massaged my tongue against hers, the sweet, minty flavor made me want to devour her. But I couldn't bear the thought of being some experiment. My brain said it was better for me not to know what it was like to have her than to know and lose her.

I pulled back, breaking the kiss. "Please don't make this hard."

"You don't want to try?" She sounded defeated, and my heart was already breaking.

"I don't even know how that looks. What does nontraditional mean to you? Because, to me, it sounds like you want to keep it a secret, and if we have to hide, it makes it feel wrong."

"No. This..." she pointed between us, "isn't wrong. It's new and exciting but also comforting. I don't understand it. But I want to explore it. I know a secret doesn't sound appealing, but when the timing is right, we'll be able to tell the world."

I wanted to believe her, but this wasn't my first rodeo. I'd been in a closeted relationship before, and she claimed we would come out, too.

The funny thing was, the timing was never right for her. But you could only keep things hidden for so long until speculation shined a spotlight on you. After a year of living together as "roommates," people started to talk, and that was the end of us. I couldn't go through that with Monica.

"I don't think I can. You have a lot on your plate, and being with me would only complicate your life. It's easy for me to get swept up in you because I think you're amazing. But I have to protect myself. I hope you understand." That was the hardest thing I ever had to say, but I knew it was the only way to keep myself safe.

"I've never been in love," she blurted out, and I stared at her, not sure where she was going with this. "I mean, I've said I love you before, but it wasn't love. I had a fondness for him and a deep liking, but it was on a friendship level. I wasn't there romantically."

"That's okay. Sometimes we want things to work so badly that we force them. But you can't always predict how it will end." I felt bad for her, but there was no way for me to know that she wouldn't look back on this and think the same.

"Exactly. So, I don't know what will happen between us, but I think we owe it to ourselves to try. Because..." she closed her eyes and let out a long exhale, "I think I could fall in love with you."

Oh my God. Those words had my brain surging with serotonin, and all my reasonableness went out the window.

"Really?" I was a breath away from her lips.

She nodded, and I was a goner. I fervently kissed her, wanting her to know I felt it, too. I opened her mouth again with my tongue, and she eagerly let me in. This woman had me on an emotional rollercoaster, but I was at the peak and didn't want to come down.

I moved with less urgency and gently nibbled on her lip. She let out a little moan, and my heart was back on the racecourse.

Finally, I ended the kiss and wrapped my hands around her waist. "So, is there a timeline for our big reveal?" If I knew she had an end date, I would feel more secure in my decision to give us a chance.

"After I get the regional position, everything will be better." Her eyes were like a midnight sky, and the light made them sparkle.

I wasn't sure that was a good enough answer, but my heart told my brain to shut up. If this was a shot at love, I couldn't pass it up out of fear.

"Okay. We better get you sorted before your segment." I leaned in, inhaling her scent, which was sweet like fruit but crisp like the ocean air. It differed from what I remembered in high school, but it still held the same power over me.

"I don't want to let you go." Her vulnerability was palpable, and I'd never known her to be so unguarded.

"Good thing you don't have to." I winked and hoped I put her mind at ease.

"Will you leave after you pick my outfit?" she asked shyly.

"Not if you don't want me to."

Her cheeks turned slightly red, and I didn't want her to feel embarrassed.

"It's okay to want me. I want you all the time." I didn't mind putting myself out there if I knew she was my reward.

"Would you? Stay?"

"Of course. Whatever you want." I'd spent my life wishing I could be the person she wanted, and now that I was, there wasn't anything I wouldn't do for her.

She audibly swallowed, and I wasn't sure what was going through her mind. "I've never met anyone like you."

Maybe that was true. She didn't know me in high school, but I didn't know her either. She had more layers than I could count and was even better than I had pictured.

"I hope that's a good thing." I smiled, but there was a seriousness in her expression.

"Please don't break my heart."

I wasn't expecting that. This was Monica Hart, high school homecoming queen, prom queen, and captain of the cheerleading squad, asking me not to hurt her. It seemed like an alternate reality—only this was my life.

"If you only knew…" I didn't finish the thought, but hopefully, it said I was right there with her.

"Let's make a deal. We won't ever hurt each other?" She held out her pinky as a promise, and I linked mine with hers.

I knew that wasn't something we could guarantee, but at least we were vowing always to try not to.

When the cameraman finally called, "and we're off," Monica was leaving the stage, but her co-host stopped her. I was too far away to hear, but I could see, and I wasn't a fan of how she was touching her.

I'd never been the jealous type, but worry drifted through my mind because Monica had never explored this side of herself. What if she only felt something for me because I was different? What if I'd given her the courage to flirt with other women?

What was wrong with me? We only decided over an hour ago to give us a chance, and I already had doubts. I shook away those negative thoughts.

When I looked up, I made eye contact with Monica, and her entire demeanor brightened, and all my worries floated away. Things were looking up, and I wouldn't self-sabotage the best thing that ever happened to me.

CHAPTER 16

Monica

PRESENT DAY

I finally wrapped up my last story and was ready to spend some uninterrupted time with Jade. But before I could leave, Joanna trapped me.

"Hey." She moved into my personal space and placed her hand on my forearm.

I didn't want to be perceived as a bitch, so I didn't back away like I usually would. "Hey? Did you need something?" I looked over and saw Jade staring, and I didn't want her to think anything, so I gave a slight finger wave and smiled at her.

"What's going on with you? You're glowing."

I brought my free hand up to my cheek and could feel the warmth. "No, I'm not. It's hot under all these lights. You know that."

She laughed but then leaned in close to my ear. "You look hot, but not from the lights."

Was she hitting on me? What the fuck? Could she tell I'd been with a woman? Would everyone know?

"If I had to guess, I'd say you had a quickie before the show." She chuckled, but her expression said she was serious.

So she probably wasn't flirting, but it still made me uncomfortable. The conversation, her nearness—all of it. I wanted to leave and feel Jade's hands on me, not hers.

"Well, you'd be sadly mistaken. I don't do *quickies*." I wouldn't have stopped Jade if she had wanted to keep going earlier, but she would have been my first.

"Are you always such a prude?"

Now she was pissing me off, so I didn't mind giving myself some distance. Pulling out of her grip, I responded, "I think privacy and decorum are things many people forget these days. If you'll excuse me, I need to get going."

She rolled her eyes, and I could tell she didn't fully buy what I was selling. I knew she'd be watching as I left, so I walked off the stage, right past Jade, without saying anything. I wouldn't give Joanna the satisfaction of starting any rumors. Jade's expression appeared confused, but she didn't try to stop me, so I hoped she knew to follow.

I didn't want any confusion, so I pulled out my phone and sent a text just in case.

Me: Meet me at my house.

As I headed toward the parking lot, I saw Scott and Tina talking. I didn't want to get held up, so I waved as I went by, but that didn't satisfy them.

"Girl, get over here. I haven't seen you in a month of Sundays." Tina hugged me so tightly that I could barely breathe.

"I saw you two days ago? You're my producer, so you're kind of hard to avoid."

"So you admit you're trying to avoid me?" she questioned.

"What? No! I was merely pointing out that I see you every day I work."

"Yes, but when was the last time we all got together?" She turned toward Scott, and he nodded in solidarity.

"I know I've been MIA lately, but we'll do something soon." I glanced at my phone and saw Jade messaged me back.

Jade: Is that a question?

Fuck! I'd upset her. I was being bossy again and not giving her choices. It wouldn't be easy for me to text her now in the middle of this inquisition. Maybe I could hit the call button, and she would realize I was being held against my will.

"Hello?" I could hear her but wasn't about to answer it.

"How about now?" Tina asked, and I heard Jade say, "Hello," again.

"Who is that? Is someone talking?" Scott stared at my phone.

"Oh? Are they? Ooops. It looks like I accidentally dialed someone by mistake." Putting the phone to my ear, I said, "I'm so sorry. I didn't mean to call you. May I call you back in a minute? I'm catching up with some friends."

It was so stupid. I should blow them off, but I felt they would know something was up if I did.

"I think I'm going to go home." Jade's voice sounded dejected, and my heart broke.

"No! I'll be right there. Bye." I hung up as if it were an emergency and hoped she knew I was putting her first. "I'm so sorry. I have to go. My neighbor locked herself out, and I have her spare key." That was a horrible lie, but I was on the spot, and it was the best I could do.

"Oh, okay. Well, you owe us a rain check then." Tina came back in for another bear hug, and I braced myself for the impact. She was small but mighty and didn't always realize her strength.

"You got it. I'll check my calendar and get something in the books. You two have fun and behave." I pointed at them as I backed away.

"Please. This one doesn't know the definition of the word." Scott hitched his thumb toward Tina, and I had to agree.

She was feisty, which was why she was such a good producer. She wouldn't back down, and if you didn't do something to her liking, in no uncertain terms, she let you know.

"All right. I'll see you soon." I rushed to my car and immediately called Jade back.

"Hello?"

"Jade. I'm so sorry. I didn't know Scott and Tina were going to stop me. And my text was a question. I mean, it was me pleading with you to come to mine?" Never in my life had I groveled so much for a person. But with her, everything felt precarious, and I wanted her to know how serious I was.

"What about ignoring me after you'd asked me to wait for you? Is that what it's going to be like? You can't even talk to me in public?"

I sighed. This was harder than I thought it would be. "I know. It was just that Joanna made me nervous, and I thought it was better not to add fuel to the fire."

"I understand you don't want people in your private life. I'm not saying we have to flaunt anything. But, fuck, Monica. You completely passed me by as if I were invisible. And you didn't even apologize but demanded I meet you at your house instead. Do you even care how that makes me feel?"

I was shit when it came to relationships—not only romantic ones. My walls were as high as my skepticism. I didn't trust easily, and I tended to see things through only my eyes. I couldn't start something with Jade and still be like this. It wasn't fair to her.

"You're right. I messed up. Please come to my house and let me make it up to you?" I knew I couldn't be affectionate in public, but I could shower her with all my attention in private. But not if we never had that chance.

"I don't know." Her voice was wavering, and I needed her to give me another shot.

"What can I do?"

"What do you mean?" She sounded wary of my offer.

"What can I do to get you to forgive me?"

She let out what sounded like a frustrated growl. "That's the thing. I feel like a fool. You fuck up, then apologize, and like a little puppy, I come running back to you. I don't think this is going to work."

A sharp pain stabbed in my stomach at the sound of her words. "I'm trying to do better. To be better. I've never had a relationship that meant something. Please don't shut me out. We can let each other know our expectations. If we don't meet those, that's when we call it. But not before we even try."

"I'm already here." Her voice was almost a whisper, but relief washed over me.

"You have no idea what that means to me. I'll be there in less than three minutes." I saw Jade leaning against her car when I pulled into my parking spot.

With her arms crossed, her body language wasn't as accepting as I had hoped, but maybe she would lower that armor once we talked.

I exited the car and waved, but she responded with a head nod. It hurt a little to see her act so cold toward me, but she also looked sexy as hell. That was an inappropriate thought to have, but with her, I was no longer in control. My brain and body did whatever they wanted without my say-so.

As I punched the numbers into the keypad to let us into the lobby, she still hadn't spoken to me. When I finally unlocked the door to my place, we went inside, and I pointed to the TV area.

"Do you want to sit on the couch and talk? I can bring up some drinks and food."

"Yeah. Sure. But I don't need anything right now." She was still standoffish.

"Okay." I needed to turn this around for good. I had to fix this and stop messing everything up. Even though I hadn't been in a real relationship, I couldn't use ignorance as an excuse.

We headed up the spiral staircase to the sitting room and kicked off our shoes before taking a seat on the chaise couch. She stayed closer to the armrest while I tucked my feet under me and faced her.

"I've never been in a relationship for myself." I knew that sounded pathetic, but it was as honest as possible.

If she was going to forgive me, she needed to know me better, and I couldn't hold anything back. Most of the time, I wanted to save face at any cost, but that wouldn't get me anywhere with her, and I knew it.

"I dated my high school boyfriend for almost two years, and he was great. But in the end, he wanted someone who made him feel something, and he said if I didn't start showing more emotion to people, I would end up living a lonely life." I understood where he was coming from, but I didn't have it in me to fake enthusiasm.

His words had stung, but they were something I needed to hear. And now, I was thankful for them because it made me realize I couldn't keep holding back or I could lose someone special.

"The thing is, I didn't love him. I was with him because everyone thought we should be. He was the quarterback, and I was the head cheerleader. It was expected that the two of us would be together, so we were." I didn't know if he felt the same pressure, but our relationship always seemed more out of obligation than passion.

"But if you didn't love him, it's good that you didn't lead him on."

That was true. Even though Damon and I had sex, I was confident he could tell my heart wasn't in it. Again, that wasn't fair to him, but I gave what I had. However, it turned out I didn't have that much.

"Then the next man I dated was in college, and my father set us up. He was conservative and 'husband' material. Everyone thought we would get married, and honestly, so did I." I closed my eyes, thinking about how different my life would have been.

"What happened?"

"I couldn't do it. As much as my parents wanted me to, I felt nothing. Dating him to make my father happy was one thing. But being with him for the rest of my life... that thought made me claustrophobic. So when he asked me to marry him, I said no."

"What did your parents say?" She turned her body toward me, and I could see the concern in her eyes.

"It disappointed them. Maybe it even pissed them off. I'm not entirely sure. But I was only twenty-two, and I wasn't ready for marriage. In the end, my dad was glad I didn't do it because potentially going through a divorce would have looked worse." I scoffed because I was nothing but a player in their game, and my happiness wasn't their top priority.

"And the other people you dated? Were they hand-picked by your parents?"

"I didn't date anyone else. I'd gone out on some dates here and there, but never the same person more than twice. The last time I'd been out with someone was three years ago."

She appeared shocked by that information but didn't say anything.

"My career is important to me, and even though I have steady hours most of the time, I could be called in on a moment's notice. So, it was easier for me not to have to worry about someone else and focus on myself." That sounded bad. "I didn't mean it to sound that selfish. I was trying to think of them, too."

She nodded like she understood, but I wanted her to know I wasn't thoughtless.

"I didn't want to be someone who couldn't give as much as the other person. Both people deserved to get something out of the relationship."

"That makes sense, and I don't think you're selfish. It's important to do what makes you happy. But what would make us different?" She stared at me skeptically. "Your job hasn't changed, so why do you think we could work?"

"Because I want us to. That's what I'm getting at. All the people before were like accessories that didn't mean much. But with you, my entire outlook has changed." I didn't know how to explain it because I'd never felt this way before.

"But not really. You still want to put your work first, and you'll always care what other people think. I'm not sure there's a place for me."

There was nothing I could do. My hands were tied, but I couldn't give up because I could see us together.

"Yes. Both of those things are true. My job is still a priority, and I worry about my parents' opinions, but neither is more important than my happiness. Before, when I had days off, I thought about work and looked for stories to pitch, but you know what I thought about this past weekend? Kissing you. Touching you. Being close to *you*." I couldn't stop thinking about her if I'd tried, but the thing was, I didn't want to.

"I have never craved someone the way I do you. Don't you get it? You've changed my outlook on everything. And I refuse to let you go without a fight because you are the entire package. Tell me what I can do to show you that I can be the person you need in your life." I was terrible at relationships, but I would do whatever it took to be who she wanted me to be.

She covered her face with her hands. "I need to feel like I matter, and I'm not sure you can do that. You have your life all figured out, and adding me would probably cause you chaos."

"It's controlled chaos, and I need *you*." I reached for her, and she didn't pull away. "I've never needed anyone before, and that's scary as hell, but I can't hold back with you. Can't you see—I'm at your mercy."

She squeezed my hand, but I could see the pain in her eyes.

"Jade, I can see you in my life. I picture us sneaking stolen kisses in my dressing room, going places—platonically—but together, and then coming back here to ravish each other behind closed doors. I know that isn't exactly how you want it, but it won't be that way forever."

She pulled out of my grasp and rubbed the back of her head. "That could work for a while, but what happens if someone finds out about us? Are you going to leave me in the lurch?"

"No!" I crawled onto her lap and brought her ear to my chest. I wanted her to hear how I felt. "I wouldn't leave you because you're the only person who makes my heart do this. And if I can't have you, then I don't want anyone."

I wasn't sure if it was me straddling her or if my words finally sunk in, but she laid me down on the couch and showed me forgiveness.

CHAPTER 17

Jade

PRESENT DAY

Monica was good at pouring her heart out to me when needed. But I wished we didn't have to go through all these issues to get to that point. I wanted her to talk to me openly all the time instead of it taking me threatening to leave before she did. The back and forth was giving me whiplash, and I worried we would end up crashing and burning before ever discovering what we could be.

But now she was on my lap with my head pressed against her chest, and I listened to the unsteady rhythm that pounded inside her. I believed she was trying and wanted to make us work, which was all I could ask for right now. Our journeys were different, but with some compromising, I believed we could end up on the same path.

I laid her back on the couch, staring into her deep-blue eyes, and found nothing but pools of desire. It felt like she wanted me as much as I wanted her, which made my body react. I ran my hands through her long hair as I slowly lowered myself to her lips, locking her in a kiss.

This was my way of sealing the deal and letting her know I was going to give us a try. But I wanted more than a kiss. I'd had those lips, which tasted so good, but it made me wonder how sweet other parts of her were.

When we were drinking, she made it clear to me she wanted to go farther, but now that we were both of sound mind, I wasn't sure she was ready for that. She'd only ever been with men, and to be her first was a big deal. She needed to set the pace, but it was hard for me because I wanted to devour her right here and now.

As we kissed, her hips rolled into me, making it harder to use self-control.

I had to come up for air before my brain completely checked out. "Do you want to—"

"Yes!" she breathed out excitedly, even though she had no idea what I was asking.

"Yes, what?"

"Yes, I want to..." She cupped my ass and pushed me into her center.

"I was going to say slow down."

"What? Noooo. I don't want that. I thought you were going to say go to the bedroom." Her eyes were full of lust, and I smirked.

Seeing her so passionate about me only fueled my fire.

As I bit her earlobe, I whispered, "To the bedroom, then?"

"Unless you want to do it here." She was hungry, and I wanted to satiate her.

"No. Let's go to bed. There's more room to maneuver." I got up and pulled her off the couch.

Before we could make our way down the stairs, I teased her with my tongue, trailing it down to the hollow of her neck. She shivered and pulled me closer, grinding her center against mine. I had to stop, or I would end up taking her on the floor.

She laced our fingers together and tugged me toward the stairs. I let her go first so I could watch her ass as she descended. She wore a black leather skirt that hugged her frame, with a see-through black top and a black camisole under it. She was always stunning, and I couldn't wait to get my hands on her.

We made it to her room in what felt like a blink of an eye, and she immediately pulled off my shirt. I didn't have to question if she was ready or not—she let me know. Standing there in my bra, I wanted to savor this moment. She reached for her top, but I stopped her.

"We don't have to rush. We have all night." The light shined in from the hall, but the room was dark. I flipped the switch so I could fully appreciate her. "May I?" I questioned as I toyed with the hem of the sheer shirt.

She nodded, and I gently lifted it over her head. I'd seen her in less before, but standing there in a skin-tight black tank top and that form-fitting skirt, she took my breath away.

"You're dripping with sexiness." I licked my lips, thinking about where I'd like to put my tongue.

She unzipped her skirt and slid my hand down to her damp center, and I felt myself throb. "I'm dripping with something." Her eyes smoldered, and I sucked my lower lip between my teeth to avoid moaning loudly.

I dragged my hand up her center as I pulled it out from under her skirt. On my way up, I took her camisole with me, and she was in just a black lacy bra. With her long, dark hair fanning over her porcelain skin, she looked like an exotic Snow White, and I wanted to explore every inch of her.

She tugged at her skirt, but I stopped her.

"Leave it." I smiled while she stared in confusion.

I reached around her back and unsnapped her bra. Both straps slid down her arms before falling to the floor, and I stared at her inviting nipples. I slowly dragged my tongue over one, watching as her breath hitched.

I lifted her skirt as I dropped to my knees and removed her panties. She watched with rapt attention, and her hand went to the back of my head.

I stared at her ideally kept center, and I could see it glistening. Sweetness exuded from her, and I was ready for a taste.

I looked up, and she tightened her hold on my head, making me think she wanted me closer. "This moment is better than I could have imagined, and I want to savor it."

An "ahhh," escaped her lips.

"Are you sure you want this?" I had to triple-check because there was no turning back. Once I started, it would be tough for me to stop. Her honeyed scent drove me mad, and I could only imagine how my tastebuds would react.

"You don't have to ask. Take me however you want because I'm giving myself to you." There was an urgency in her voice, and I felt the need.

"I hope you enjoy the ride." I nipped at the inside of her thigh as my hands massaged up her legs.

When I arrived at her apex, my thumbs made their way to her wet lips. When I touched her for the first time, she jerked back a little, and I gazed up at her only to see her eyes fluttering shut.

"Do you want to watch?" I questioned before dragging my tongue up her fold, and her eyes popped open.

We stared at each other as I slid a finger inside. She breathed a "yes" as she pushed her hips toward me.

"Do you like it when I'm inside?" I knew she told me to take what I wanted, but having her enjoy it was all that mattered.

"Yeah. Put another finger in." This was the only time I wanted her to boss me around.

It was a huge turn-on knowing what she liked. She pulled my head closer as I worked two fingers in and out of her. She didn't have to say a word. I was more than happy to oblige.

I sucked her clit in my mouth, and she let out an "ahhh, yes." I loved the sounds and wanted to hear more. I curled my fingers inside as I glided my tongue up and down her folds. She gripped my hair every time I hit a spot she liked, and it drove me wild.

I wanted to taste her, so I removed my fingers and pushed her onto the bed. I pulled her legs over my shoulders and dove tongue-first inside as her wetness dripped down my chin. The deeper I went, the louder she got.

"Jade. Oh, yes."

Hearing my name only sent me into overdrive. Her skirt slid over me as I moved harder and faster.

Her legs clenched my shoulders, and her hand stayed firmly intertwined in my hair. She held onto it like a rein and wasn't letting me go—her wanting this so badly only added to my arousal.

I never thought this could happen, but it was even more intoxicating than I'd imagined. I brought two fingers to her clit and rubbed small circles over it while I continued showering her with my tongue. That pressure must have been what she wanted because every part of her tightened, and she grinded her center into my face.

Sweat was trickling down my back, and I loved every minute. My tongue spun around like a cyclone, and I wouldn't stop. She was breathing so hard, I could barely make out her words, but it sounded like keep going, so I did. I wanted her to ride the wave as long as possible before taking her to the next peak.

When her hands loosened their grip on my head, I figured she was on her way down, but she had no idea we were far from done. I took my fingers and drove them deep inside her. I continued ravishing her, and she perked up.

"Oh my God. I already came," she said raggedly.

"Trust me. It gets better with each one." I swirled my fingers around as I moved them in and out.

I stood up and placed one knee on the bed beside her, giving me better leverage to hit her most sensitive spots. Plus, I wanted to see her chest rising and falling faster as I continued.

"That feels so good, but rub my clit." She directed, and her command caused goosebumps to cover my body.

I dragged her wetness up her fold and began sliding my fingers around her pleasure zone. With each circle, she arched her back and screamed.

"Yes!" Her hips bucked, and I could tell it wouldn't take long for her second one. "I want your mouth on my tits."

"Yes, ma'am." I dropped down and captured her nipple between my teeth, sucking it with force.

Her hands held me in place like she did when I was between her legs.

"Move to the other one." She pushed my head to where she wanted me to go.

As soon as I nibbled on her taut nipple, she started clenching. I kept stroking her clit while I consumed her tits.

"Ahhh," escaped her mouth like a guttural sound. "Jade."

Finally, I let her float down as I lay beside her with my head on her chest. I peppered her breasts with kisses and continued reveling in her sweet juices.

She exhaled loudly as she tried to catch her breath.

"Wow! Just... Wow!" She relaxed. "You're the first person who ever gave me an orgasm."

A smirk crossed my face, and I was glad she couldn't see. "Oh yeah? Well, that was only act one."

"Oh, no. I don't think I could go again. Besides, I haven't even seen you." Her fingers played with my hair.

I looked up to see her staring down at me. "You'll see me when I'm riding you."

Her eyes widened, and she bit her lower lip.

"This is an intermission, but then it's on to the final act. Only to be followed by an encore. You won't remember anything about your previous lovers by the time I'm done."

I stood up and urged her to lift her hips as I ripped off her skirt. Then I stripped down, ready to show her a night that would be burned in her mind forever. I wanted her only to have memories of us.

CHAPTER 18

Monica

HIGH SCHOOL

I couldn't believe it was time for prom. Since Damon and I had broken up, I was going with Jeff, another guy on the football team, but I wasn't excited in the least. He was a neanderthal and wouldn't know good taste if it bit him in the ass. But he was the "next in line" behind Damon in popularity, so it was a given that he and I would go together. High school was about over, and hopefully, when it ended, so did these preconceived notions of how I was supposed to live my life.

Tara, Patty, Ashley, and I were getting ready at my house, and the guys were meeting us here. My dress was pale purple with a deep V in the back and a high-necked front. With a mermaid-style waist, it hugged my hips, fanning out as it reached the floor. Mine was the least revealing of everyone's, but I chose that purposefully.

The last thing I wanted was to put ideas into Jeff's head. In my mind, I was going with him more out of obligation than a good time. If all went well, we would only dance to a couple of songs. Then I could blow him off and do my own thing.

I knew that sounded horrible, but I couldn't stand the thought of him pawing over me all night. Most guys had a hard time taking no for an answer. That was one thing I would miss about Damon. He never pushed me, and if I were going with him tonight, I wouldn't have to worry about anything except maybe holding his calloused hands.

"This is going to be so much fun. I can't wait until the afterparty," Tara squeed as she finished applying her makeup while we all waited.

"Of course you're excited. You're going with Paul, and he's gorg." Patty almost sounded jelly, but she was going with her boyfriend, so I wondered if they were having problems.

"Oh, like Nick isn't cute, too. We have scored the hottest guys in school. I think we should all be happy about that," Ashley chimed in, and I smiled and nodded.

I couldn't give two shits less about this dance, the afterparty, any of it. As soon as cheerleading was over, I was done with all their drama. Getting away from their pettiness would be a highlight about leaving high school. That and moving out of my parents' house. Being in this petri dish was suffocating, but complaining about it would make me sound even more entitled.

"Are you bummed that you're not going with Damon?" Tara turned toward me and smirked like she hoped I was.

"Damon and I have been over for months now. I've moved on. But I know you like leftovers, so you should go for it with him." I gave a fake-smile and realized they were all staring at me like I'd kicked a puppy.

"Sorry. I'm on my period. Besides, you could do better than Damon, anyway." I shouldn't have lied to smooth things over, but I needed to keep the peace.

"It's okay. I figured as much. You're looking bloated." Tara waved her hand in front of my body, and I immediately regretted feeling bad about what I had said.

But she had low self-esteem, so I would let her have this. "You know it. And I'm crampy. Add some zits, and it would be the trifecta."

"If I'm honest, it looks like you might be getting a pimple on your nose. Hopefully, it won't show on the pictures." Tara had to keep digging, but I could be a bigger person.

I didn't need to drop to her level to feel good about myself. "Fingers crossed."

"Okay, ladies! It looks like your dates have arrived. Come down so we can document this night," my mom called to us.

"Coming," I responded as I got up and headed toward the door.

Ashley and Patty led the charge, and Tara and I were the last ones out.

"You're never going to win," she mumbled.

"Excuse me? Win what?" I grabbed her arm to stop her.

"You think you're perfect, but everyone sees right through you. You're scared of everything and will never win at anything because you can't even stand up for yourself." Her words felt like a slap to the face, but I wasn't about to let her see that she affected me.

"Well, I've been winning at life just fine. And I will always come out better than you because I'm not a bitch who has to tear people down to feel better about myself—that's you. So, while you're stepping on everyone else to get to the top, I'll already be there, living my best life."

Without batting an eyelash, she swung around, and her open hand connected with my cheek, stinging like hundreds of tiny needles poking me. But I kept my face neutral and my head high.

"Fuck you, Mon. I don't need to be in your shadow anymore. This world is almost over, and so is your reign. I hope you enjoy tonight because it will be the last time anyone fawns over you. You may have been a big fish in a small pond, but once you leave, you'll be a minnow, like everyone else." She turned on her heel, leaving me standing there speechless.

Maybe she was right. I wouldn't stand out in the real world, and I could be myself, flying under the radar. She might have thought that was a diss, but it sounded like a dream come true to me.

(Present Day)

"Good morning, gorgeous," Jade purred into my ear, and I rolled toward her.

"Good morning yourself. You seem chipper. What time is it?" I blinked, hoping I didn't look as tired as I felt.

"Eight o'clock." She brushed the hair out of my face and smiled at me.

"Eight? In this house, we don't get up before noon. Go back to sleep." I pulled her closer, but she immediately climbed on top of me.

"Well, sleepyhead, some of us have to do things before the bats wake."

"That's not fair. You kept me up until the break of day. How are you not tired?" I stared at her, and she had this mischievous grin.

She pressed her hips into me, and my body remembered her touch and craved more, but I knew I couldn't handle it. That was the most action I had ever seen in my lifetime, and it happened in one night.

"I am tired, but I also have tons to do, so I don't get to stay in bed all day. But if I did..." She leaned down and sucked on my earlobe, and I suddenly didn't care that I was sore—I wanted her now.

"Do we have time to..." I tilted my head back, exposing my neck, and she moved her lips down like I'd hoped she would.

As she traced her tongue along my collarbone, goosebumps broke out, and I wasn't tired anymore.

"Not this morning. But tonight, be ready," she growled against my skin, and I had full-body shivers.

I ran my fingers through her hair, tucking it behind her ears to see her. "You're the best thing that's ever happened to me."

She kissed my forehead, then my nose, then my lips. It was a peck at first, but I deepened it, massaging my tongue against hers. She hummed into my mouth as she nibbled on my bottom lip.

"You are going to make me late," she breathed out.

"Late for what? I thought you were your own boss."

"Ha. I am, but that doesn't mean I don't have clients to answer to. You know I'm trying to start a clothing line. I have to ensure everyone I deal with is satisfied so they will support me when I get it off the ground." Her expression went from lustful to anxious, and I could tell how much this meant to her.

"There is more to it than knowing how to sew. You also need to have business acumen and good client relationships. Therefore, I have to go. But I'll see you at the studio at four. Unless…" She raised her eyebrows, and my mind went there—sex in my dressing room.

"We have to behave. You know that. I want this to work outside my house, so we need to do it right." I'd always been bad at relationships, but this one felt different, and I didn't want to blow it up because she made me hornier than a teenage boy.

"I know, I know. Don't worry about a thing. I hope you have a good day, and I miss you already." She gave me one more kiss before getting up and putting her clothes on.

Watching her dress was almost as sexy as watching her undress. She wasn't curvy, but she was feminine. I couldn't put my finger on what I enjoyed the most because she was the entire package. Her confidence, personality, aura, eyes, lips… those lips. It was like they were made for me the way they fit perfectly with all parts of my body.

"No patting the bunny while I'm gone. I want to be the only one who touches you." She smirked.

If she thought my "bunny" would let me pat her, she had another thing coming. It needed rest, just like me.

"You're funny. Me and my bun bun will go back to sleep and anxiously await your nice, gentle strokes."

"Hmmm. Who says I'm going to be gentle?" She quirked an eyebrow, and that perked Thumper right up.

"You have to go before I rip your clothes back off." I blew a kiss to her, and she acted like she caught it and put it on her mouth.

"See you soon. Lo—Byeeee." She rushed out the door.

That was weird. I wondered what she was saying, but I didn't dwell on it too long as my eyes drifted closed.

At 11:30 a.m., my phone went off, and I rolled over to see what it was—a text from my mom. She told me I needed to meet them for lunch next weekend for Spencer's promotion. Argh. That was the last thing I wanted to wake up to.

Even though I felt exhausted, I got out of bed and went to the bathroom. I needed to get ready and do some things around the house. While I let the water heat up in the shower, I checked my emails and saw one reminding me to RSVP for our fifteen-year high school reunion, which was happening in a few months.

I'd completely forgotten about it, but there was no way I was going. I had so much to handle right now, and being around all those fake people would only bring me down. Besides, I knew Tara and the other girls from cheerleading would be there, and I couldn't be fucked with seeing them. The last time I had spoken to Tara was the night of prom. Now I can't even remember what the falling out was over, but I remembered her slapping me, and that was the end of us.

As I climbed under the warm rainfall, I tried to think of my good times in high school, but they were few and far between. Even though Damon and I didn't work out, I was fond of him and our time together. Then I wondered what had happened to that Mystique girl he had a crush on. Maybe she was his wife now. Stranger things could happen.

I laughed because, the day after graduation, I had left all those people behind me and hadn't thought of them since. It served me no purpose to reminisce about a time I wished had never happened, but I couldn't help and wonder what everyone was up to. Maybe I needed to know I made a good choice by cutting ties with them, or perhaps I was just curious if they had changed.

After rinsing off, I got out and blow-dried my hair as I stayed firmly on memory lane. When I was done, I ran to my closet and pulled out a box that held my high school memorabilia. Grabbing out my yearbook, I flipped through some of the pages, looking for anything that would make me miss that place. When I came to our senior pictures, I read what everyone wrote for "Where Do You See Yourself in Ten Years."

I saw Damon's first, and he said, married with children and working as a pilot. At least he was living some of his dreams. I wondered why he chose law instead, but I probably wouldn't ever find out. Oh well. As long as he was happy, that was the important thing.

I kept looking until I found mine. I wanted to be a cardiologist who married another doctor. Well, I missed that mark by a long shot. But I was happy where I had ended up, so it was probably for the best.

Then I checked out Tara's, which said she would be an actress living in California. Last I heard, she was a PA to an associate producer. It didn't sound like she would ever find her way onto the big screen. But it wasn't that surprising. Her personality probably shined through, letting people see the ugliness within.

As I was closing the book, someone caught my eye—Mystique. She stared at me with her hair hanging over her eyes, covering most of her face, and her quote, "I want to be an artist who inspires others to see the beauty in everything."

That thought made me smile. I hoped she accomplished her goal and found a place to fit in. She had a rough go of it.

I scanned back to her name: Mystique Miller. Then I stared at the only thing showing in the picture—her black lips. She was a non-conformist, and I envied that. But as I studied those pouty lips, a sense of déjà vu flooded my mind.

"Good morning, gorgeous." Jade's face danced around my head... "I don't get to stay in bed all day. But if I did..."

Oh my God. Was Jade... *Mystique*? There was no way she didn't know who I was. I talked about high school, my family, and *Damon*. She let me go on and on, pretending to be unaware.

It felt like my world was bottoming out. Last night was one of the best nights of my life, and it was all based on a lie. How could she do that to me? An even better question is, why?

My eyes studied every little piece of her picture, and all I knew was that Jade had some explaining to do.

CHAPTER 19

Jade

PRESENT DAY

"Aren't you all rainbows and sunshine? Who is this person, and what have you done with my friend?" Iris teased as we sat in Joe Joe's, drinking coffee.

I'd texted her to meet me because after leaving Monica's, I knew I would need some caffeine to make it through the day. Also, I wanted to share my news. I didn't know I could feel this good, yet here I was, smiling so much my face hurt.

"Can't I be happy?" I questioned.

"You can be. I've just never seen you like this. What happened?" She took a sip of her coffee, awaiting my response.

I wanted to keep her on the hook, but I was too giddy. "You remember that woman I was telling you about? The one I went to high school with?"

She nodded in acknowledgment.

"Well... we're dating." I was like a kid at Christmas—I couldn't hide my excitement.

"Oh my God! That's great! She finally recognized you?"

A pang of regret coursed through me because I hadn't mentioned it. But I couldn't imagine that it would bother her. It would probably be more of a laughable moment.

"Not exactly. But it doesn't matter because she has gotten to know me for who I am, which is so much better. Otherwise, she might not have given me a shot." I wanted to believe I was justified in my actions, but how Iris narrowed her eyes over her coffee mug made me second-guess myself.

"What? Why are you looking at me like that?"

"Um... Well... I would never judge you, Jade. But don't you find that a little dishonest? You had prior knowledge but didn't offer to share?"

"Right. I mean, I knew who she *used* to be. But I've gotten to know the current her, and my feelings are on a different level than they were when we were younger. It was purely a physical attraction in high school, but that's not the case now. She is deeper than I thought. She's funny, smart, and a little bossy, but I like it."

She smiled, but I could see there was concern in her eyes. "That's great. I'm thrilled for you. But you plan on telling her, right?"

I shrugged. "I don't think it's relevant. We're already together. What good would it do?"

"How long have you been together? Have you *slept* with her yet?" She might not have wanted to judge me, but her tone was laced with disapproval.

What difference did that make? We talked about our expectations and what a relationship would be like. Never once did she ask me about my past. If she had, I might have said something. But, to be honest, it was a time I'd rather forget.

"We officially got together last night. And..." I gave her eyes, hoping she knew what I meant without having to say it. I wasn't the type to discuss who I was with, but I knew Iris was trustworthy and had my best intentions at heart.

"Shit, Jade. That makes it worse. It looks like you lied to her so you could... *get in her pants*," she mumbled at the end of the sentence, but I could make out what she said.

"What? No way! Me not saying anything had nothing to do with her. It was about how I felt. I've grown so much since high school, and I didn't want to return to that insecure and hurting person. I would never lie to her."

"Well... you withheld the truth, so... *isn't* that a lie?"

"No. It's not my fault she didn't remember me, and I remembered her. If the tables were turned, I wouldn't care. The thing is, she had the high school experience you'd be jealous of. She was rich and beautiful and popular. I was none of those things. I doubt she even knew my real name."

She sighed and reclined in her chair as she ran her hand over her face. "How she grew up doesn't matter. It doesn't make her less deserving of the truth. I feel like you're making excuses because you don't want to discuss it. Are you afraid she wouldn't like you now because of who you used to be?"

I hadn't consciously thought of that, but it was a possibility. After spending four years being bullied, I had a different outlook on life. I could let it break me down or strengthen me, and I chose the latter. The girl who used to let people walk all over her was no longer here. She said goodbye when I started going by my middle name. Mystique no longer existed, so there was no need for Monica to remember her.

"It doesn't feel like a lie. I've reinvented myself, and this is destiny. We lived very different lives but ended up in the same place. The fact that we found each other is all that matters, and I think she would agree." I hoped that if I said it enough, I would feel more confident in my answer.

She leaned forward and slid her chair out. "Okay. I got to get back. Hales will need help when the kids wake up. But please think about giving her the chance to decide what is and isn't important information, yeah? I want you to be happy, but if it's built on deception, it will all come crumbling down. I know from experience."

I stood up and hugged her goodbye. Then I grabbed my not-even-half-drank coffee and tossed it in the trash. I couldn't finish it because I felt sick to my stomach.

The day was so busy that it passed by before I knew where it went. It was already 3:30 p.m., and I was on my way to the studio. I'd given Iris's suggestion some more consideration and decided she might have been right. Even though it didn't matter to me that I knew Monica previously, it might matter to her, and I had to give her the chance to choose.

But the longer I contemplated it, the more worried I was that she would end things. There was no way Monica Hart would end up with the likes of Mystique Miller. She was in the majors, and I wouldn't even be in the stands. But we weren't those people anymore. Could Monica Starr and Jade Miller make it?

I wanted to have faith that the past was in the past and the future was all that mattered, but Iris had made me feel like I was doing something wrong by not saying anything. I couldn't continue to be silent if there was a chance it would hurt Monica. She was way too important to me.

I didn't deceive her on purpose. At least not consciously. I put very little credence into who she was when we were younger and focused on who she was now. And that person was someone I was falling in love with.

As I walked into the studio, I saw Scott looking stoic as he stood outside Monica's dressing room.

"Hey, is everything okay? You don't normally camp out here." I questioned, but he shushed me as he steered me away from the door.

"Something's going on with Monica. She came in puffy-eyed and told me not to talk to her. That's not like her at all. She always at least asks me about my day." His words caused my heart to race.

I couldn't imagine what had happened between my leaving and now, but I was worried. All I wanted to do was be there for her, but I couldn't rush off, or he might think something was up.

"Weird. Thanks for the heads-up. I'll keep an eye on her... for you," I quickly added.

"Good luck. I've never seen her this upset. Let me know if you all need anything." He patted me on the back and headed back to his stand.

"Thanks, Scott." I returned to her room and knocked, but there was no answer. When she didn't reply, I burst through the door to ensure she was okay. But I found her lying on the love seat with a magazine in hand. "What are you doing? Why didn't you answer?"

Her head turned so slowly that she looked like a puppet. Without saying a word, she went back to her magazine.

"Are you okay? Scott said something was wrong. Talk to me." I rushed to her side, but she held her hand like a stop sign.

She sat up and stared at me. "Is there something you want to tell me?"

There was, but now wasn't the time to bring that up. I worried my bottom lip for a second, trying to figure out where she was headed with this. "I want to make sure you're all right. Did something happen? You were delighted before I left."

She tilted her head from side to side. "Yeah. Something happened." She didn't elaborate, and I searched her face for clues but came up empty.

"Okay. Am I supposed to guess, or will you fill me in?"

She was obviously on edge, and I wanted to help, but she was making it nearly impossible.

"If you don't have anything to say, this conversation is over. Pick out my clothes, please. I have to be on set in forty-five minutes." She got up, walked to her makeup chair, and started fiddling with her hair.

"If *I* don't have anything to say? You are the one who is upset, and I want to listen. You know how much I care about you, right? I don't want to see you like this." I didn't understand where this coldness was coming from.

She stared at me in the mirror. Her eyes were as dark as the night sky.

"I guess you should have thought about that, then." What was she talking about? Thought about what?

I had been here for less than five minutes. What could I have possibly done?

"Babe. You're not making any sense. Please, talk to me." I swiveled her chair around to face me, and tears trickled down her cheeks. "What's going on?"

"Why don't you tell me, *Mystique*."

Holy shit. I'd royally fucked up.

CHAPTER 20

Monica

PRESENT DAY

"What? How did... You remember me?" She stuttered words, but at least she wasn't trying to deny it.

Not that it made it better, but lying would have made it worse. Although I honestly didn't think there was anything she could do to fix this.

"Yeah. I mean, no. I didn't realize you were her until I saw your picture in the yearbook today. But there is no way you didn't know who I was, especially when I was talking about the past. So I'm very curious why you kept that to yourself." I narrowed my eyes as the hurt flooded my body.

"Was it like a revenge thing? We didn't get along in high school, and now you were going to fuck me and leave me? You're going to run and tell everyone that I'm gay? What exactly is your endgame?" I was at her mercy, and I felt defeated.

I'd spent so much time protecting myself that I never really enjoyed life. Then, the one time I let my guard down, I ruined everything. There was a reason I wanted to be alone—no one could hurt me.

She reached out her hand but stopped when I crossed my arms. "No, I would never tell anyone anything you confided in me. I have no ulterior motive because I genuinely like you." Her eyes were heavy, and she took a deep breath. "In fact, when I was leaving this morning, I almost said I love you. How could you think I would be so cold?"

I scoffed. "How could I not? You pretended like you wanted to get to know me when you already did. What were you doing? Gathering intel to... I don't know... sell to other news stations so you could start your fashion line?" That may have been a bit much, but I'd never been this hurt.

She probably wasn't such a devious mastermind, but she had some reason for deceiving me, and I didn't want to stick around to find out. There was too much she could use against me as it was, and I couldn't allow her more ammunition. I needed to jump ahead of this before a scandal occurred.

"You have to know me better than that. I have integrity. It was an error in judgment, and I'm sorry. If you think about it, isn't it kind of funny?" She chuckled, but all I could see were my dreams flying out the window, and I wanted to scream.

What the fuck? My life was in her hands, and she was laughing.

"There's nothing funny about this. You're a liar, and who knows what else? I can't have you here. You're fired." I turned my chair back and watched in the mirror as her mouth hung open.

"What? You don't even want me to help you anymore?" She appeared hurt, but her feelings were misplaced. She had no claim to that emotion.

"No. And I'm calling Scott in here and telling him how you hit on me. That way, I have a witness on my side when you go to the press." It made me sick to slander her, but I had to cover my ass.

"Wow. Here I thought I was falling for this amazing woman when really you're a devil in disguise. You don't need to tell Scott anything. Have an NDA drawn up, and I'll sign it. I'd prefer not to have my name run through the mud for no reason other than I made a mistake." She looked like she was fighting back tears, but she'd made her bed, and now she would have to lie in it.

"For what it's worth, I'm sorry. But I didn't say anything because I was protecting my emotional well-being. High school might have been your glory days, but it was hard as fuck for me. Being true to myself caused me a lot of pain. But I'd rather be alone and proud than fit in being someone I'm not."

She wiped her eyes, but my heart was too broken to feel sorry for her. I had told her things that no one else knew. And to find out she knowingly lied to me and then slept with me made me feel used.

"All right. I'll have my producer bring one in. But after you sign it, you need to leave. I can't be near you." I called Tina, and a moment later, she had the paperwork at my door.

"Hey, girl. You know how it works. I'll stay here and notarize it if you both want to sign it." She glanced over at Jade, then lowered her voice so only I could hear. "Does she know something?"

I usually told Tina everything because she helped protect me, but this wasn't something I was ready to spill. "You know we have anyone working with me sign them. It looks like this one got through the cracks. But she agreed to sign it now, and I don't think she's said anything before, so it should be effective."

"Okay." Waving over my shoulder, she beckoned Jade to come. "All right, ladies, you need to sign here and here and initial here." She pointed to three separate places on the page. I did mine first, and Jade followed suit. "Perfect. I'll get these processed and scanned into the system. Now get ready, so we can have another killer segment." She gave me air kisses on both cheeks, snatched the papers, then scooted out.

"Do you want me to pick your outfit before I go?"

I'd never heard her voice so shattered before, but I couldn't let her stay, or I might give in.

"No. I'll manage today. Scott will walk you out and get your badge." I moved toward the clothing rack as she headed toward the door with her head down.

Before she left, I called out, "Jade." She spun around with tears in her eyes, and I could feel mine returning as well. "I asked you not to break my heart. I fucking hate that you did."

"Well, if it's any consolation, I broke my own, too." This time she left, and I didn't stop her.

Picking up my hairbrush, I threw it across the room. "Goddamn it!"

I didn't want to cry. I had to be on set in thirty minutes, but there was no use. The tears flowed freely, and I sat down and let them. After a ten-minute breakdown, I wiped my eyes and took a couple of deep, relaxing breaths. The show must go on.

I wished my real life was scripted, so I wouldn't have to deal with this hole in my chest.

I hadn't seen or spoken to Jade in five days, but it seemed like a lifetime. It was weird how close we'd gotten in such a short period, but when you finally showed your vulnerability to someone, it caused an immediate connection.

I was disappointed that I had opened up, but at the same time, it had felt so good to let someone in. I was being true to myself and no longer playing a part, and it was freeing. And if I was honest, I missed it—*I missed her.*

But I couldn't let myself go there. I had too much to do, and wallowing over what could have been wouldn't change anything. So I pushed down all of those feelings and started getting ready. It was my brother's promotion lunch, and I couldn't be late, or my mom would never forgive me.

I'd already fixed my hair and makeup, so all I had to do was slip on my cocktail dress and sandals. When I arrived at Café Paris, I did a once-over in the mirror and was confident no one could tell I had been on a sadness bender for the last week. As I exited the car, I checked my phone. I was there before the allotted time, which was one less thing for me to stress about. But when I walked inside, I saw everyone sitting and enjoying an appetizer.

"Monica! You're late," my mother hissed out. "And why are you wearing that? You know this is a fine-dining establishment. You look like a streetwalker."

Everyone's eyes turned toward me, and my cheeks heated in embarrassment. "This is a cocktail dress, which is suitable for a lunch gathering. I'm sorry if it isn't to your liking, Mother. Next time, I'll consult you before leaving." I gave a closed-lipped smile, and my brother shook his head, warning me, but I didn't heed his advice. "And for the record, I'm not late. I'm ten minutes early. Unless you changed the time."

"I said 11:00 sharp." She stared at me, and I kept my face neutral.

"No. You said 11:30, and it's only 11:20. Therefore, I'm early."

"Well, if I said 11:30, why is everyone else here already?" she quipped back, and my jaw clenched, but I realized she had a point.

Since I didn't want to turn this into a bigger argument, I conceded. "You're right. I'm sorry I had the time wrong. I'll do better." That appeared to appease her, and I congratulated Spencer before sitting next to my father.

"Daddy. How are you?" I put my napkin on my lap, and he poured me a glass of white.

"Well, I'd be a hell of a lot better if all these people would stop bringing frivolous cases to my courtroom." He took a drink, and I studied him. He had a big presence and an even bigger voice.

I felt sorry for anyone who had to go before him. I knew firsthand what it was like to be judged by him. If he disagreed with your side, he wasn't one to listen to your argument. I was sure he was more fair on the

Bench. But in my life, there was no convincing him otherwise once he had his mind set.

"Oh? What kind of suits?" I questioned curiously.

"You know. There have been many defamation and discrimination cases, and they are basically a he-said-she-said type of thing. Unless you have physical evidence, keep the drama at home." He shook his head in annoyance.

I understood some of them were hard to prove, *but* if someone was wronged, it was important for them to be heard. "Not all those cases are trivial. People deserve to have a voice. Surely, you can agree with that?"

"Well, you wouldn't understand because you don't have an important job. But when I'm constantly dealing with cases like that, I can't help the people with actual issues." Wow! Everything about that statement was offensive.

I couldn't let it go. It was one thing to put me down, but it was another to ignore that people were being wronged for reasons out of their control.

"Actually, Father. You may not realize this since you're a rich, straight, white male, but discrimination and defamation are serious crimes, which need to be punished."

He sat up, and anger flashed in his eyes. "Are you telling me that I don't understand the law?"

"No. I was merely stating that you're privileged. Therefore, you see things differently than those who have lived a less fortunate life."

He let out a belly laugh, and I couldn't figure out what was so funny. "That's a good one. You're a bit of a pot, huh? You don't think you've had a charmed life? If it weren't for me, you wouldn't have gotten the anchor job."

He blew a raspberry between his lips. "Don't be so high and mighty, Monica. Being a rich, straight, white woman isn't considered a minority, either."

I closed my eyes and inhaled deeply before slowly releasing it. "Right. I know I've been blessed, but you have no idea what you're talking about. I have to be twice as good as the men anchors to get a third of their pay. I work my ass off at my job, trying to find leads and stories and even help with producing." My voice wanted to crack, but I steadied myself before continuing.

"And if you want to take credit for me, fine. I don't need you to be proud of me because I know my worth." I was shaking because I wanted to say so many other things, but I knew now wasn't the time. Turning toward my brother, I said, "Spence. I'm sorry, but I'm going to head out. I'm not feeling so well."

"Sit your ass down. This is a family lunch, and you're staying," my father boomed, but I was past the point of caring.

I already felt like shit because I missed Jade, and I didn't need to stay here and listen to his arrogant ass tell me who I was. He couldn't have been more wrong in his assessment, but I wasn't ready to introduce him to his real daughter yet.

Without waving goodbye to anyone, I scooted out of my chair and headed to my car. All I wanted to do was curl up in bed and read a book. I only wished Jade was there to hold me. Why couldn't my mind let her go?

CHAPTER 21

Jade

PRESENT DAY

The Gala was in a couple of weeks, and even though Monica wasn't speaking to me, I figured I'd finish her dress so at least Mr. Banks would pay me. Since I wasn't working at the station anymore, I didn't have that extra cash flow, and my savings account wasn't growing as quickly as it had been.

As I worked on the final touches, my heart was aching at the thought of not seeing her in it. She was going to turn every head in the room, and I hoped she didn't give in and go with that tool bag. He didn't deserve to have her on his arm. She was a princess in her own right and definitely didn't need some wannabe prince exploiting her.

I would give anything to be the person who shined the spotlight for her, but I wouldn't even get to see her in the dress, and it tore me up inside. But I couldn't have a pity party because I was the only one to blame.

Even though I didn't realize my withholding the information would cause that reaction, I couldn't be mad at her for her feelings. I had to own up to my actions and accept the consequences, which was why I was trying to make amends.

By her lack of communication, I could tell she wasn't interested in giving me another chance, but I could only hope that dropping off the dress would at least show her I would always have her back, even if we weren't together. I knew her place was under lock and key and no one would let me in, so I thought my best bet would be to take the dress to the station.

After wrapping it in a box, I headed to Channel 13. I figured I could have Scott deliver the package for me. He didn't know what happened between Monica and me, but he was a good guy, and I hoped I could count on him.

But when I arrived, I saw something I wasn't expecting—Monica. She was sitting in her car alone but appeared to be talking. Maybe she was on the phone. I couldn't be sure. I didn't want to interrupt, so I waited a couple of minutes. However, she continued, so I approached and tapped on the window.

"Fucking hell!" she screamed, and I dropped the box. "Jade? What are you doing?" She opened her window as I picked up the present.

"I brought you something." I held it out to her, but she stared at it skeptically, like she thought it was a bomb or something. "It's your dress... for the Gala." She still didn't reach for it, so I said, "Do you want me to put it in the back seat?"

"I already bought another dress. You can keep it." She was matter of fact, and her coldness sent shivers through my body.

"Okay. You don't have to wear it to the Gala, but maybe you want it anyway? I think it would look amazing, and I want you to have it."

"I'm sorry your work was for nothing, but I'm not interested." She started to roll up her window.

"Wait! I know I screwed up, but please..." I didn't know what I could say to change her mind, so I left it with that plea.

"Please what? Forgive you for making me out to be a fool? Well, I'm all out of forgiveness, but I have a pocket full of fuck yous." She replaced her hurt with anger.

"I was never trying to play you for a fool. I didn't want you to remember me the way I was in high school, and I thought this could be our fresh start."

"But it couldn't be a *start* because you already had a leg up. So all those times you said things that didn't add up, it was based on your prior perspective of me. You weren't giving me a blank slate. You kept your mouth shut for your benefit, not for 'us.' I opened up to you, but you never once did the same."

I hung my head because she was right. My fear of losing her held me back, and ironically enough, it was what caused her to leave.

"May I sit?" I pointed to the passenger seat, and she shrugged before sort of nodding, so I took that as my shot. I rushed around the car and climbed in, setting the box in the back. "Please give me a chance to explain?"

"I gave you a chance, Jade—several chances. But you refused to offer me anything other than an apology." Her eyes swirled with emotion, but I waited because I knew she wasn't finished. "I understand we had a different high school experience. But it wasn't all tits and gravy for me, either. I was vulnerable with you, and you could have been the same with me, but you *chose* not to."

"I know that! Don't you understand? I was scared that you would realize you were too good for me, so I thought if I pretended that the past didn't exist, we might have a future. Maybe you would see me for who I was today—a confident person looking for my better half." I swallowed hard, hoping not to get choked up.

"I didn't want to be that insecure teenager who pined after you but would be nothing more than a freak in your eyes. Do you know I heard that word so much from your friends that I believed it was true?" The tears were coming, but I didn't fight them. She wanted me to pour my heart out, and I wouldn't hold back.

"But I know better now. I changed that voice inside my head, and returning to that person didn't seem like an option. And when you didn't remember who I was, I thought maybe we could get to know each other on a different level." I looked up at the roof, hoping the tears would stop falling.

"I never thought you were a freak," she all but whispered, and I closed my eyes. "I know I didn't stand up for you, and I should have, but I never believed what Tara or anyone else said. I thought you were brave."

Her fingers squeezed my leg above my knee, and I flinched. She pulled back, and I wanted to kick myself for scaring her away. I needed her close to me. Her touch was like a bandage on my broken heart, and it felt like forgiveness, which was more than I could ask for.

"I'm not near as strong as you, but I wish you would've given me the chance to show you I'm not the person you thought I was, either. You had me in a box without allowing me to show you all the sides of myself." She let out a deep exhale.

"I know. You're so much more than I ever imagined." I had been so worried that she would judge me for the past that I didn't notice I had done that to her.

"When I was younger, I was scared to rock the boat, so I kept quiet. My brother was Mr. Perfect, and my parents expected nothing less than that from me. And now, I realize that made me a coward. I don't want to be remembered that way, just like you don't want to be remembered as the outcast. We are both growing and deserve the chance to spread our wings."

I was now looking at her, and it was like her words caused a metamorphosis because she was no longer Monica: homecoming queen, Ms. Popularity, or my high school crush. She was this incredible woman who was just trying to be better than she used to be. She was asking to be seen for the person she'd become, and we weren't as different as I had believed. I grossly underestimated her.

"I don't want to hold you back. You have come a long way, and I know you have more you want to do. I hope you know I'll always be in your corner." I sighed and felt like a weight had been lifted off my chest.

"And I hope you realize that you've been a big part of my growth. How you call me on my bullshit has made me more aware of my actions."

"So, where does this leave us?" My eyes fluttered, and she offered me a sad smile.

"I think we need to find ourselves before we can expect anyone else to recognize us."

I didn't quite understand that, but I knew enough to realize it meant we weren't getting back together. "Okay. You will always be a happy memory to me." I sucked my lower lip into my mouth.

"This doesn't have to be goodbye. I think we could still be friends," she offered, but the word "friend" felt like a nail in my coffin.

"Sure." I fought back the sadness from my voice. "Keep the dress. I gotta go." I darted out of the car before the floodgate in my eyes opened.

Her seeing me like that was more than I could bear. I'd shown vulnerability but still didn't get the girl, so it was time to go home and lick my wounds.

It seemed like no matter how much I wanted to change my path. I ended up in the same place—alone.

CHAPTER 22

Monica

PRESENT DAY

Jade rushed out, and I stayed and reflected on what had happened. I appreciated her honesty—finally. But sometimes, things came too late. I wasn't mad at her, though. At least now I understood why she did what she did. Although it didn't change my opinion—I still thought she was in the wrong.

Once I saw her drive away, I exited my vehicle and headed inside. I was now running late, and I hoped no one would notice. When I entered, I saw Scott, who waved me over.

"Oh my God. Tina was about to call a search party. Is everything okay?" He studied me, and I rolled my eyes.

"Yes. I'm fine. I had to take care of some things—no big deal. But now I need to get ready. Ciao." I blew him a kiss, pretending like everything was peachy. There was no reason for me to alarm him.

"Okay, but I need to give you a heads-up—" he called out, but his warning was too late as my mother bombarded me as soon as I opened the door.

"Where have you been? I've been trying to get hold of you for over an hour!" She was frantic, and I had no idea why she was here. It was so unlike her to come to my work.

"Calm down. I must have kept my phone on silent and forgotten to turn it back on. Where's the fire?" I moved toward the wardrobe because I had to multitask to make the segment in time.

"The fire is your insubordination. Did you know someone taped your little outburst at lunch? And then posted it all over social media, making your father look like a bigot?"

Oh, shit. This was the last thing I needed.

"I'm sorry. I didn't know that happened. What can I do?" I couldn't handle a fallout with them right now.

She huffed as she crossed her arms but didn't offer a response. I continued shuffling through outfits until I saw the one Jade had made, and my heart sank. I hadn't given it back to her. As I stared at it, I remembered the moment when I realized how attracted to her I was. My fingers brushed across the material, and I had a pang of regret that she wasn't here with me.

Maybe saying we could be friends wasn't the right thing. Even though I wasn't ready to jump back into bed with her so quickly, my body ached for her touch. My thoughts were more than friendly, but I had to hold my ground.

She'd screwed up, and me acting like I wasn't hurt wouldn't make the pain go away. The irony of it all was that she was still the only person I wanted to be near.

As I thought about her and us, I had completely zoned out to my mother's rant.

"And you're going to fix this because his job could be on the line," she finished.

"What? Tell me what to do, and I'll do it." I slid on a red sequined top with black slacks and heels. I was in a dark place, and my outfit would reflect that.

"Well, I think you need to apologize on-air for your actions and say that the video was taken out of context."

Was she kidding me? I wouldn't take airtime to talk about a personal matter. That wasn't how my job worked. I couldn't highjack the segment for my family drama. And to be honest, I hadn't said anything that wasn't true. He was the one who stuck his foot in it—not me.

"I can put out a tweet saying we are a privileged family who wants to help be a voice for the voiceless, but it feels like our hands are tied." Even that made me cringe because I knew it was a lie. No one else in my family gave a shit about the little people.

She appeared disgusted. "That isn't good enough. You need to make a statement tonight on the news so everyone can see how regretful you are that your words were twisted."

"No. I can't do that. I won't risk losing my job over something that wasn't my fault. Daddy said what he said. So if he is receiving backlash for it, there isn't anything I can do."

She was fuming, but I didn't have time to deal with this.

"Mom. I have to get ready. I'm late. We can discuss this when I get off work."

"There's nothing to discuss. If you don't make the public apology, you're done." Her words sounded final, but I didn't understand her meaning.

"Done with what?"

"Done with the family. Your father has already written you off, but I told him I could fix this. However, you're making it impossible. So, what's it going to be?" She tapped her foot as if it were a timer, but I shut down.

Their conditional love wasn't anything I needed in my life. Everything I did was out of fear that they would do this exact thing. I was done with their games. It was time to take my life back.

I picked up my cell and dialed Scott.

"Hello, Ms. Starr. What can I do for you?"

"Hi, Scott. Could you please come to my room and escort my mother to her car? I have to get ready for the show, and she needs to leave."

She stared at me, shooting daggers from her eyes, but I merely smiled in her direction.

"Um. Okay. Sure. Be right there," he stumbled out the words, and I felt bad for getting him involved, but she needed to know who was boss.

"You're kicking me out? You can kiss this job goodbye. It will only take one call from your father, and you'll be gone."

"If he is the only reason I have this job, fine. I don't want it anyway. But I am confident that I've earned my position on merit. So do your worst and see what happens. I'm always going to bet on myself because I deserve it."

A second later, Scott tapped on the door before entering.

"Mrs. Starr, may I walk you to your car?" He reached out his hand, but my mother turned her nose at it.

"My last name is Hart, and no, you may not. I can see myself out." She pushed past him, and I waved for Scott to follow.

He was quickly behind her, and I closed the door. This day couldn't have been more emotional. Hopefully, I could get through this segment without having a breakdown.

I tried to cover my anxiety with makeup and a confident attitude, but I was a wreck. Once I got dressed and headed to set, Joanna immediately cornered me.

"Why are you so pale? Are you sick?"

"No. But apparently, I look like shit." I huffed.

"I didn't say that. You just look different. Is everything okay?"

I never understood if she cared or was fishing, but either way, I wasn't opening up. "Yeah. I'm good. Are you ready?"

She studied me for a minute, then sat down. "Let's do this thing." She clapped her hands together and smiled broadly, but I wasn't sure what she was so excited about.

As the lights brightened, the cameraperson shouted, "Ready in ten, nine, eight, seven, six..." and then counted on their fingers to start.

Shock crossed my face when the camera cut to a live feed showing riots outside my father's courthouse. There were protestors holding signs saying, "Peace not Prejudice," "Justice Isn't a Privilege—It's a Right," and "Bigots Don't Belong Behind The Bench."

I turned to Joanna, who was grinning like the Cheshire cat, and I felt sick. She knew this was going to happen and didn't warn me. The camera zoomed in on me, and I wasn't prepared. I stared at the footage and then went back to the teleprompter.

"There was a video leaked of Judge Hart..." I swallowed hard because how was I supposed to report on a story involving me?

I felt like I was going to have a panic attack. The lights were getting hot, and my chest was getting tighter. I tried to focus on anything else, so I scanned the room until my eyes landed on *Jade*? What was she doing here? She stood next to Scott, looking as horrified as I felt. There was no way I could continue, but it was like I was frozen.

The cameraperson realized I wasn't going to speak, so they toggled over to Joanna, who took over the story. Once she finished highlighting the lunch and commenting on how the protesters wanted Judge Hart to step down from his position, they cut to commercial while Jade came rushing up to me.

"Monica. Are you okay?" Concern laced her voice, but I didn't answer. "Did you know that was coming? Because you seemed pretty surprised."

I shook my head but still couldn't find words.

"Wow! Watching your face was a show itself." Joanna came over to us, and Jade had a fire in her eyes.

"Did you know that was going to happen?" She didn't even give her time to respond before getting in her face. "Did you?" She had a "don't fuck with me" tone, and Joanna appeared scared.

"Who the hell are you?" Her voice wavered a bit, but Jade didn't back down.

"I'll be your worst nightmare if I find out you set this up. Now, tell me, did you know they were going to kamikaze her?"

"Look, Rambo Barbie. I was merely getting a headline. I had no idea they didn't tell her. Don't shoot the messenger." Joanna held up her hands, and Jade's jaw tightened.

The way she had my back made me melt. Even though we weren't anything to each other, she was protecting me. It appeared she was the only person I could count on in my life.

"The fact that you would sell out your co-host to try to further your career makes you a disgrace," Jade spat out.

"Whatever. She would do the same. So you can point that judgment somewhere else. I don't regret anything." Joanna smirked, but as fast as lightning, Jade's fist connected with Joanna's face, knocking the smile right off.

"Oh my God." I finally found my voice as I watched Joanna cup her nose with her hands.

"You bitch!" she screamed out, and Jade shook out her hand as if it hurt.

Scott came rushing to the stage and grabbed Jade, leading her away. I watched as the cameraperson started counting us back to live. I turned toward Joanna, covered in blood, and realized it would be on me to finish the segment.

Unfortunately for the station, Jade had given me some of her backbone, and I was no longer going to sit here and take this. I stood up as I pulled out my earbuds and removed my microphone.

"Sit down... we're live," Tina hissed from the sidelines, and I couldn't believe I'd ever thought she was my friend. She completely blindsided me with that story, and now she wanted my help.

Fuck her, fuck this place, fuck it all. My entire life was a shit show, but all I was worried about was if Jade was okay.

As I dropped my equipment on the table, I held my head up and walked proudly off the set. I knew it probably meant I would lose my job, but at this point, I didn't care. Nothing about this life was my own, and I was ready for the fresh start Jade had talked about.

Things weren't going the way I wanted, so it was time to make a change. I was taking my power back, and if I had to start over from the bottom, so be it. I was tired of crawling on eggshells. I was ready to fly.

CHAPTER 23

Jade

PRESENT DAY

"Jade, I'm so sorry, but I have to call the cops," Scott said as he detained me in this small room. "I'm sure Joanna deserved it, but she wants to press charges."

I rolled my eyes. I couldn't go back in time and unhit her, so I had to take my punishment on the chin. "I get it. It's okay. I know you're only doing your job."

Before he could put in the call to the police station, someone knocked on the door.

Scott strolled over, cracking it just enough to see who was there. "Oh, hey. Come in."

Monica walked inside and saw the ice pack on my hand. "Oh my God. Are you okay?"

"Yeah, I'll be fine. Just a battle bruise." I smiled, but she didn't appear amused. "You're upset. I'm sorry. I know I fucked up again." I hung my head, so I didn't have to see her disappointed face.

"Scott, could you give us a minute?" Monica asked as she sat down next to me.

"Yeah, but you have to be quick. Joanna wants to press charges, so I have to get a statement to the police ASAP."

"I understand. Thank you." She waited until he left and then tilted my chin toward her. "I'm not mad, Jade. You stuck up for me, and no one has ever done that before." Her eyes were full of compassion, and I was sad that everything went down the way it did. "How did you know?" She tucked my hair behind my ears, and I leaned into her hand.

"After I left the station, I drove by the courthouse and saw the Channel 13 van parked outside with the protestors. I pulled over and went up to the crowd. They were chanting unsavory things about your father." I didn't feel the need to pour salt in the wound, so I kept the specifics to myself.

"Then I heard the cameraperson tell them to call their friends and get more people there so they could be on TV. Nothing about it seemed right, so I came back. I had Scott paged, and I explained what was going on, and he let me in. He thought it must have been a misunderstanding, but he allowed me to stay. And well, you know the rest."

She stared into the distance, and her eyes darted around as if trying to add things up in her head. "You're telling me that the station provoked them?"

"That's what it sounded like. They wanted to create a spectacle." I knew Joanna had something to do with it, which put her on my shit list.

Monica was so private and did everything she could to keep her life out of the limelight, and Joanna blew that up in a matter of minutes. She was lucky I only punched her in the nose. She deserved a full ass-kicking.

I could see her brain working it all out, but she didn't say anything more about it. "I'm going to put in a call to Trent. He should be able to take care of any charges brought against you. Then I'm going to do some digging on Joanna. There is no way she has a clean past if she did something so sneaky."

"Don't call Trent. I don't want him to think you owe him a favor. He might expect something..."

I figured she could fill in the blank. I wasn't sure if she got the same creepy vibe as I did from him, so it was better if I kept my mouth shut. Even though it would be nice if I could get out of this predicament, I wouldn't let her risk her hide to save mine.

"I can handle him. The main thing is that we keep you safe." She squeezed my hand before lacing her fingers through mine, and my heart started jumping in my chest.

What was she doing? Did she realize this would make me feel things —*think things*? She'd said she wanted to be friends, but I wouldn't hold my friend's hand like that. My eyes studied her, but she wore her poker face like a champ.

As she leaned in a breath away from my lips, the door skidded open, and she immediately jumped up as Scott entered. We were no longer in the bubble that was keeping us close. We were in the real world again, where we weren't meant to be together.

She wanted to grow on her own, and she needed to find acceptance of herself before she could accept someone else. Living her life for other people had made her feel lost, and I understood she would need time before she could be free from those chains. It made me sad.

When we were together, we were pretty fucking amazing. I believed we made each other stronger, but it didn't trickle down to our everyday lives. She still feared judgment, even from Scott, who was supposedly her friend.

I hated that she was closed off. If she let people in, I knew she'd have much more support than she imagined. But she didn't see the world the same, and I couldn't change that.

"All right, I gotta make that call." Scott appeared remorseful, but I smiled to let him know it was okay.

"Don't worry about it. I texted Senator Banks, and he said he would handle it." Monica chewed on her bottom lip and wouldn't make eye contact with me.

"Why did you do that? What does he want in return?" I wasn't happy that he would think she was in his pocket now.

"He didn't say. He only told me he would handle it. It's going to be fine." She turned to Scott. "Can we go now?"

"Um. Let me call the chief of police and see what he says. I trust you took care of it, but I must cover my ass. You understand?"

Poor Scott. I didn't want him in the middle of this. "Yes. Please call. It's your job." I stood up and walked toward Monica, who was in the far corner. "Don't do anything to compromise yourself for me," I whispered.

"Oh, you're a fine one to talk, Ms. Mike Tyson. You were protecting me, and it's my turn to protect you." She rubbed her finger across the back of my hand. "It's what we do."

Scott cleared his throat, and we both turned around. He stared at us, and it looked like his cheeks turned a little pink, but I couldn't be sure it wasn't just the lighting.

"The police chief said there would be no charges. I didn't ask any further questions, but you're free to go."

"Thank you." I came closer and shook Scott's hand.

"I didn't do anything, but you're welcome. Could you hang back a second?" He asked me and then looked at Monica as if silently urging her to leave.

"Okay. Well, I'm glad it's all handled. Um, I guess I'll go then." She appeared hesitant, then scooted out the door, leaving it cracked.

Scott walked over, tapped it closed, then looked at me.

"Is everything okay?" I was worried by his expression.

"Monica is my friend."

"Okay? She seems very fond of you." I didn't know where this was going.

"She doesn't let many people in, so you must be special to her. If you fuck her over, I'll ruin your life." His words were a shock.

"What? I'm not special to her. I hardly know her. Please, don't—"

Monica burst through the door, cutting me off mid-sentence. "That's not true. You know me better than anyone. And I don't care if the entire world knows—I'm falling for you." She grabbed my hand while Scott stared—only he didn't appear as surprised as I felt.

"I'm proud of you, Mon." He threw his arms around the both of us, making it a group hug, but I stood there stiffly, unsure what was happening.

Monica had gone from zero to a hundred faster than I could snap my fingers.

I tried to get my thoughts in order, but I needed clarification. "What about all that stuff you said in the car? About us finding ourselves? What about your parents or your promotion? How has so much changed in such a short time?" I rapid-fired questions, but my head was spinning.

Scott released us and said, "I'm gonna give you two a minute alone." Then he rushed out the door as if his ass were on fire.

"I realize that my life before wasn't my own. I lived according to everyone else's expectations and still got shit on. You were the only person who didn't want anything except for me to be happy." She stared at me with a twinkle in her eyes.

"Shit, you even punched someone in the face to defend my honor. You are the only person who cares for me, and I need to make decisions with your interests in mind, not all those other people who would never have my back."

This all seemed too good to be true. Was it possible I could get my happy ending? I guess there was only one way to find out—give her *another* chance.

CHAPTER 24

Monica

PRESENT DAY

"You are the only person who cares for me, and I need to make decisions with your interests in mind, not all those other people who would never have my back." I pulled Jade closer and wrapped my hands around her waist.

"So what do you say? No more secrets. No more games. This is our official fresh start?" I quirked my eyebrow in that questioning manner. I hoped we could finally get things right this time, but we had to be on the same page, or there was no point in trying.

She appeared to ponder my proposal, and I worried she was about to say no. "Does no more secrets include telling people about us?"

"Yes," I said without hesitation.

"And what exactly would we say we are?" She tilted her head, and I hated she put me on the spot, but I hoped my answer would be what she wanted to hear.

"I would like to call you my girlfriend."

She looked up to the ceiling and tapped her lip with her index finger like she was thinking, but she had a smirk on her face, which told me she was messing with me.

So I decided to give it right back to her. "It's fine. I take it back. We should probably just be friends. I mean, there was *zero* sexual chemistry between us. I don't know wha—"

Without letting me finish my thought, she cupped my face and crashed her lips into mine. I moaned into her mouth as I missed this feeling. Everything about her turned me on, and if we weren't in Scott's office, I wouldn't be able to stop myself from ripping her clothes off. But before I could get past the point of no return, I pulled back.

"So, is that a yes?" I licked my lips, savoring her sweetness a little longer.

"I would've waited. But if you're sure this is what you want, I am more than ready. There is no one I have ever wanted to be with more. Even when we were younger, I was taken by you. And that has only grown tenfold since I've gotten to know you." She beamed.

"I've waited my whole life to find someone who makes me feel like you do, and I'm not going to let you slip through my hands again. Come on. Let's get out of here." I laced my fingers through hers and tugged her toward the door. When I opened it, Scott jumped back and leaned against the wall, pretending to do something else besides eavesdrop.

"Oh, hey. Everything good?" He wasn't stealthy, as the phone he was "looking" at was upside down.

"We are better than good. And thank you for being you. You're the only genuine friend I have." I hoped he knew how much he meant to me.

"I want to clarify that I had nothing to do with that ambush. And had Tina said anything to me, I would have warned you. But she's dead to me." He slid a finger across his throat, and I chuckled.

Letting go of Jade's hand, I reached out and gave him a bear hug. "You're the best. And I didn't see her betrayal coming, either. She was quite the actress."

"So, what are you going to do now?" he questioned, and I looked at Jade, and my body started heating up.

"I mean work-wise," Scott clarified, cutting through my thoughts. "Are you going to stay here?"

I hadn't thought that far. I was so worried about making sure Jade didn't end up in jail that I wasn't concerned about my career. That was the first time I'd ever put anything above work, and it made me realize how messed up my priorities had been.

"Maybe I'll take a break from it all." I glanced at Jade. "I have more important things to focus on right now."

"I would talk to Tomas. There's no way he cleared that stunt Tina pulled, and you know he likes you." Scott appeared a little sad at the thought of me leaving.

Even though Tomas was kind, he was still the news director, and I was pretty sure ratings would be high for this episode, so he probably wouldn't be inclined to reprimand anyone. Ratings were ratings.

"Thanks, Scott. I might do that. But even if I leave, I'll still be in touch. You know that." I winked at him, and he gave me a small smile.

"Yeah. But it won't be the same. Anyway, you two get going. I'm sure you have a lot to discuss. I'll let you know if I hear anything."

"See you later." I waved.

"Bye. Thanks for not sending me to jail." Jade patted him on the shoulder, and we headed out.

When we were out of earshot of him, I whispered, "Do you want to go back to my place?"

"Of course I do." A smirk played across her face, and my center started throbbing. "You want me to meet you there? I have to make a stop first."

"Oh yeah, okay. Sure." I wondered where she was going, but I wouldn't ask. If she had wanted me to know, she would've told me.

"I won't be long." She acted like she might give me a hug or even a kiss, but realized we were still in public and thought better of it.

I knew we had some things to work out, but I hoped it would be natural for us to do those things one day. However, today wasn't that day.

I waved goodbye as I went to my car and drove home. My house was a little messy, so at least I would have a chance to tidy up before she came. When I got inside, I put my heels away and immediately changed into sweats and a T-shirt. If all went as planned, I wouldn't be wearing them long anyway, so I might as well be comfortable beforehand.

Even though I didn't cook, my kitchen was a disaster. I had to-go coffee cups sprawled all over the counters, as well as some mail and receipts that needed to be filed. The last week I'd spent wallowing, so I didn't take the time to keep things picked up.

After making the place presentable, I grabbed a bottle of wine from the fridge and poured a couple of glasses. She'd made it sound like she would be quick, so I thought this would give it time to breathe but still be chilled.

As I took my first sip, the buzzer went off, and I jumped up to let her in. I answered the call, but it was my mother's voice greeting me.

"Monica, we need to talk."

"Mom? What are you doing here?"

"Let me in. You have some serious explaining to do."

What the fuck? I didn't think I needed to explain anything. It was pretty clear what had happened, and I had nothing to do with it. I was just as dumbstruck as they probably were.

"Come up." I huffed out, then panicked, hoping she would leave before Jade arrived and had to see all this drama.

The door opened, and my mother walked in. Everything about her radiated anger—her mannerisms, her expression, even her walk.

"Look, Mom. I have company coming over, and I don't have time for this. The station waylaid me with that story, so you can go after them, not me." I held up my hands in a back-off fashion and sat at the table, away from her negativity.

Tonight, I only wanted to focus on Jade and me, and this was putting a wrench in those plans.

"They are trying to get a petition signed to have the legislature remove him from the Bench. Is that what you want? All of this happened because you couldn't just sit quietly and eat a peaceful lunch with your family. Now he looks like a bigot, and they are saying he is too biased to be a judge." She crossed her arms and clenched her jaw.

"I'm sorry. But I didn't say anything untrue. As a matter of fact, he was the one who started it. I can't change what happened, and the footage is already out there." I loved how I was to blame for someone else's actions, but I was over it.

"Besides, I think I'm quitting the station anyway, so I'll be useless to you. And if I recall our earlier conversation, you and Daddy were already done with me. So asking for favors seems a little offensive." I was getting good at standing up for myself. Who knew I had it in me? I certainly didn't.

The buzzer sounded, and my mother stared at me, daring me to answer it.

"I told you I was busy, so we're finished with this conversation." I brushed past her and let Jade up, but I couldn't warn her about what she would be walking into.

In a matter of seconds, the door opened, and Jade was holding what appeared to be a pair of underwear and a box, but I couldn't make out what it was.

"Hey. I swung by—"

"Jade, have you met my mother?" I interrupted, and she immediately looked up and tucked her hands behind her back.

I must have been right about the panties, but I was curious about the other thing.

On the other hand, my mother didn't seem as interested but more annoyed. Hopefully, she didn't see anything and would leave us in peace.

"Who are you?" She stared accusingly at Jade, and my heart ached that she spoke so hatefully to her.

"I'm Monica's stylist. I was dropping some things off for her to try." Jade's cheeks were pink, and I couldn't help but smirk.

"Was that lingerie?" Apparently, my mother had caught a glimpse.

"What? No? That was mine. Um, I was going to change before I went out. She mentioned she was tense, so I brought over a massager. I'm sorry. I'm going to leave." Jade was so flustered it was endearing, but I wouldn't let her flounder around anymore.

"No! Mother. You need to go." I pointed toward the door, and Jade came further inside but kept her goodies out of sight.

"I'm not leaving until we figure out how *you'll* fix this." My mother's voice was demanding, but she no longer had a hold over me.

I walked to her, placing my hand on her back. "There's nothing to discuss. I already told you it is what it is, and Daddy can take care of himself. He doesn't need me to fight his battles. Isn't that what he always told me when I asked for help?"

I urged her toward the door. "Now, I'm going to give you the chance to leave peacefully, but if you don't, I'll have you escorted out again."

"Don't patronize me. I brought you into this world, and I will not be treated like a child."

"If the shoe fits." I gave her one more nudge, and she shook my hand off her as she waited in the doorway.

"You're not my daughter," she stated scornfully, but I hadn't felt that way in a very long time, so the words didn't cut as bad as she'd hoped.

"That's probably a good thing because Jade's not my stylist. She's my girlfriend." I pushed the door closed in front of her face and locked it.

"You're a disgrace," she called out, but it didn't faze me.

When she disowned me from the family, I thought it would devastate me. Little did I know I'd feel free. I no longer had to give a fuck, and her judgment didn't hold any weight.

"Thank you!" I shouted back as I stared at Jade, whose eyes were darting back and forth between the door and me. "Let's go to my room. I don't want to subject you to any more of this."

"Hold on." She grabbed my hand. "Are you okay?" Her touch was calming, and the concern on her face made me fall even deeper.

"I will be." I stepped closer and let my lips gently graze hers. "Are you going to tell me what you brought?" A smile tugged at the corners of my mouth as I tried to peek around her back.

"Maybe."

I pulled her to my room and shut the door. Whatever Jade was hiding, she must have thought I would enjoy it because she repeatedly put me first. She was the only person who cared about my happiness, and it was like the rest of the world faded away when we were together.

CHAPTER 25

Jade

PRESENT DAY

"**A**re you going to tell me what you brought?" She looked at me curiously, but now I was questioning if she would be interested.

"Maybe..." I wasn't trying to be mysterious, but I needed to read the room first.

She'd just fought with her mom, and on top of that, she came out to her. That was a lot to handle, and I didn't want her to be in a bad headspace if we were going to be physical. I wanted her to be present at all times, and if her mind was elsewhere, that couldn't happen.

"Why, maybe?" She walked toward me and reached around my back, but I wrapped my arms around her, keeping my goodies hidden.

As I held her in my arms, I stared into her eyes. She didn't appear sad, but until I knew how she was doing, I couldn't take any other steps.

"Do you want to talk about it?" I questioned.

She tilted her head. "Talk about what's behind my back?"

"Babe. I'm serious. A lot went down in less than five minutes, and I'm afraid you haven't processed it yet."

She rubbed her hands up my back. "Actually, she and I already had this fight once today. I've processed all I needed to. My parents are never going to love me for me. They love the idea of me as the perfect daughter. But when I didn't fit that role anymore, they wrote me off." She shrugged in that what-can-you-do sort of way.

"Wrote you off? What are you going to do?" I couldn't believe how nonchalant she was being.

"Well, before I met you, I would have crawled back, begging them to forgive me for things I didn't even do." She pressed her hips against mine, and my body involuntarily responded to the friction.

"But you let me open up without judgment, and I realized I don't need them. You said you'd rather not have friends if you had to be fake. Well, I'd rather not have to walk on eggshells to feel loved. I know they are 'family,' but toxic is toxic no matter where it comes from. For my well-being, I'm better off without them." She squeezed me, and a sense of calmness radiated off of her.

I believed she was okay with the way things had turned out. She put my worries to rest, and I wanted to be a safe place for her. I kissed her forehead.

"So, you're sure your head isn't somewhere else?" I needed direct confirmation.

"My mind and body are right where they're supposed to be. Now. Tell me what you brought." She tried to turn around and see, but I moved them.

Once again, my hands were behind my back, and she faced me with a less-than-impressed expression.

"I already know what it is," she bluffed.

"Oh? Enlighten me." I grinned, and her face appeared even more annoyed.

"It was panties. I saw them." If she only knew.

"Yeah? And what did you think?"

"I didn't see them that closely. But I'm curious why you brought them."

"So you didn't see the other thing?" I quirked a brow.

"Will you tell me? You remember where my head was? Well, it's starting to move away from there," she threatened, and I laughed.

"Okay. Okay. No more teasing." I brought my arms to the front, holding out the harness briefs and the box with the dildo.

Her eyes widened as she realized what I had. "Oh. Is that... I'm sorry, what is that?"

I should have known this might be a bit much. She'd never been with a woman before me, so she wouldn't be familiar with this type of thing.

"It's a strap-on, but if you don't want to use it, we don't have to. I want to give you every experience."

She reached out, took the box, and removed the dildo. "So, you put this in there..." she pointed to the underwear, "and then..." she let that hang in the air.

"Yes. Is that something you would be interested in?"

"Can we try to find out?" She appeared curious but also a little nervous.

"Whatever you want, I want. The only thing that matters is that you're comfortable and happy. And if we start, and you don't like it, you can say stop. I want us to be able to explore everything together without limits."

She took the toy and ran it over the center of her sweatpants, and I bit my lip in anticipation of me being inside of her.

"Have you done this before?" For the first time since I'd known her, she appeared shy.

"I have." I wondered if that put her at ease or turned her off.

"And you liked it?" she questioned.

"Yes. But we don't have to try it if you don't think you will."

She licked her lips. "Do you think I could wear it?"

Oh wow. I wasn't expecting that. "I've never been on the receiving end so it would be a first for me, too."

She grabbed the panties from my hand and examined the O-ring as if trying to figure out how it worked.

"If you want to put them on, I can help you get the toy in place." I smiled at her puzzled expression.

"Are you sure you want me to do this?" Now it was her turn to see where my head was at.

"I told you. I want to experience everything with you." As I leaned in, I pressed my lips against hers—softly at first, but she pushed back with an urgency that let me know she was ready.

Her enthusiasm made me ache, and I brushed my hand over her center. She let out a moan as she broke the kiss and removed her shirt. Her perky breasts were begging for attention, and I obliged.

I bent down, wrapping my lips around one of her taut nipples while she tangled her fingers in my hair. Then she directed my head to the other breast, and I willingly went. My hands went to the waistband of her sweats, and I shimmied them over her hips. She let them fall to the floor before kicking them out of the way.

My eyes drank in her body, and I locked on her wet center. With one finger, I dipped it into her pool, and she gasped. I wanted to drop to my knees and feast on her, but tonight I would let her take the reins, so I settled for a taste as I sucked the juices from my finger.

"You drive me wild," I breathed out, and she pulled me closer.

"The feeling's mutual." She licked my lip before giving it a nibble. "Give me those briefs." She slid them on, and I helped position the dildo in place.

As she stood there wearing the strap-on, she looked like a fierce goddess, and I couldn't stop staring.

"It feels a little weird having this between my legs. But I kind of like it." She stroked the toy in her hand, and it was strangely arousing.

"Yeah? I'm glad you like it. You look sexy as hell." I placed my hands on her hips, and she got a stern look on her face.

"Get undressed. Now." Her bossy side was coming out, which only turned me on more.

I did as I was told, taking off my jeans and T-shirt, but I waited for my bra and underwear. I thought she might give me more commands if I was a little defiant.

She quirked a brow as she moved in closer. The toy brushed against my center as she reached around and unsnapped my bra. I pressed down on the hard silicone, loving how it felt against me.

I grabbed her hips, rocking them into me.

"You like it?" she breathed in my ear.

My eyes were hooded, and I couldn't even get a word out, so I nodded.

"Take off your panties and tell me how you want it." Her voice was demanding but confident, and there was no way I would last long.

Her giving orders in my ear was enough to push me over the edge.

I removed my underwear and kicked them to the side as the toy stroked my pussy.

"Lie down." She bit my ear, and I moaned.

"Okay." I moved to the bed and sprawled out, waiting for what would come.

"I want to be on top, watching while I'm inside you."

I felt my juices dripping out, and I was more than ready.

She straddled my legs, stared at the toy, and then at my center.

"It's okay. I'll help." I smiled at her reassuringly, and she came down slowly. My hands guided the dildo inside, and her hips sank into me. "Ooo," I called out.

"Does that hurt?" She stopped for a second, but I gripped her hips, urging her to continue.

"No. No. It feels good."

"Okay. How do you like it? Fast? Slow? Deep?" Everything she said sounded good to me because it was her.

"Just do what feels natural to you, and I'll let you know how it feels for me."

She held herself up with her arms, and we locked eyes while she rolled her hips slowly. She stared between us as she continued moving, and I rested my hands on her ass.

"If you want, you can put all your weight on me. You don't have to stay on your arms." I thought it might be more comfortable for her, but I also wanted to feel her body against mine.

As she rested her arms next to my head, her breasts caressed mine, and I let out another moan. With my hands setting the pace, I encouraged her to move faster. That was all the prompting she needed, and she was back in control.

She forcefully captured my lips with hers as our bodies rocked together. Her tongue entered, dominating me, but I happily let it. I wanted this night to be about her and what she wanted to do. It was her time to be in charge and feel powerful.

Pulling back just enough to breathe, she said, "You are so sexy. And when you moan like that, it turns me on."

"Well, I can't keep quiet when you're inside me." My heart was racing, and I couldn't believe how lucky I was that she wanted to be with me.

"Oh my God. Hearing you say that is going to make me lose it. I'm so wet right now."

"So am I." I chuckled as the toy slid in and out with ease. I could feel my walls tightening around it. "And the faster you go, the better it feels."

"Yeah?" Her breathing picked up as she rolled her hips into me. "Like this?" She made quick, long, fluid strokes.

"Yes, like that." My head relaxed back, and my eyes briefly closed. "Keep going, but I'm going to slide my hands between us. Okay? I want to rub myself while you move in and out of me."

She raised on her arms again, and watched my hand slide down to my entrance, dragging some of my wetness to my clit. I went to work while she continued her steady rhythm. As I rubbed small circles around my pleasure zone, I could feel myself fast approaching take off.

Then, she brought her head down to my ear and whispered, "Come for me," and I was flying high.

"Yeah. Yeah. I... Go... Ooo... Monica. Yes!" A whole string of nonsense escaped me, but I didn't care. I had no self-restraint at the moment. I let myself get lost in the sensation, and it was exhilarating. It wasn't just a feeling. It was a mind-and-body experience.

When I rode out the wave, I removed my hand, and she fully collapsed onto me. Our hearts were pounding like drums, and we were both gasping.

"Wow. My arms are like jelly." She laughed. "That was quite the workout. I used muscles I didn't even know I had."

I brushed her sweaty hair away from her forehead and kissed it. "You are the best I've ever had." I let out a satisfied exhale. "I'm usually the giver, but I'll let you do anything you want."

"Oh yeah? You ready to go again?" She suddenly got her second wind.

"What?" I studied her, and she slowly moved her hips into me. "That feels good," I moaned.

"I'm pretty sure you were the one who said two back-to-back was the way to go."

"That's for you. I'm a one-and-done type." I smiled.

"So you're done for the night?" She sounded disappointed.

"Oh, no. I haven't even started. It's your turn now."

I rolled us over, leaving the toy inside me as I topped her. Her eyes widened when I lifted my hips, then slowly glided down, letting it fill me up.

"Holy shit, that's sexy as hell," she uttered, and I was ready to give her an out-of-body experience she wouldn't forget.

We'd been on a very long ride, sometimes solo, sometimes as passengers, but my favorite was as co-pilots. I hoped the future felt as good as this moment because I never wanted this to end.

CHAPTER 26

Monica

PRESENT DAY

The day of the Gala had finally arrived, and I was dreading it. I lay in bed with Jade, but Trent wouldn't stop messaging me. He still thought I was his plus one, even though I repeatedly told him I wasn't.

Trent: I'll send a car for you at five.

I sighed as Jade kissed my neck.

"What's that look for? Do you not like it?" she questioned.

"No! Of course, I like it. I hate that Trent keeps texting me about tonight. He is sending a car."

"Oh yeah? A limo? Or just a Town Car?" She scrunched up her nose, and I swatted her.

"It doesn't matter. He thinks I'm his date."

"Well..."

"Don't well... He has no reason to assume I'm going with him since I clearly told him I wasn't." I gave her a pointed stare, and she tilted her head.

"But was it clear?"

"What do you mean? I said I was no one's arm candy and would show up alone. How is that confusing?"

"But if you're alone... He might think that means you're available. Did you say the words 'I'm not your date.'?" She had a point.

"Argh. I shouldn't have to be that blunt. I'm polite, you know."

"Are you?" The corner of her mouth curved into a sexy half-smirk that drove me crazy.

"Woman. You'll be on the list if you don't stop."

"The naughty list?" she asked in a throaty voice.

"Remind me again why I love you?" I gave her an eyebrow.

"That's easy. Because I make your knees weak and your panties wet."

"You're so cocky. But I could say the same thing to you." I slid my finger up her slick center.

"Of course you could. But I never questioned my love for you." She was so ornery, and I wanted to kiss that grin off her face.

I rolled on top of her, sucking her lip into my mouth before gently nibbling it. "That will teach you."

"You think that's a punishment? You're sooo mistaken." She pinched my ass, and I squealed.

"Whatever. I have to shower."

"Oh? Is that an invitation?" Her smile was back and bigger than ever.

"No. I don't have time for that now. I have to get ready."

"For your date?" She laughed, and I tweaked her nipples.

"Ouch!"

"Did that teach you a lesson?"

She rubbed her breasts. "Yes. I'm sorry. Please don't do it again."

"You know there's a fine line between pleasure and pain, and you skate across it all the time."

"True, but that jumped the line and firmly went into hurt-like-a-bitch territory." She was now downtrodden, and I rolled my eyes.

"Oh my God. You're such a baby. Here. Let me kiss it and make it better." I leaned down and swirled my tongue around her nipple. Then I wrapped my lips around it, giving it a little kiss. I did the same on the other side. When I was done, they stood proudly, begging for more.

She gave an appreciative groan, and I didn't want to leave the bed.

"Ugh. You make it so hard to go." All of a sudden, I had the best idea. "Come with me?"

"To the shower? I already asked, and you put the kibosh to it."

"No. To the Gala." It was perfect. It could be our coming-out party, and it would keep Trent away.

"You've lost it. You know everyone will be there. People from Channel 13 are covering it. They will for sure have eyes on you. Tomas has been begging you to come back since he fired Tina. So you'll be the center of attention." She was right, but I didn't care.

"I'm not going unless you're on my arm."

"Babe, you can't *not* go. I made that killer dress for you, and it deserves to be seen."

"Then come with me." I gave her my puppy-dog eyes and saw her waver.

"Are you sure? What if it gets reported on? Are you ready for that?" Her voice was full of concern, but her opinion was the only one I cared about.

I pinned her arms above her head and stared at her. "I'm ready for the entire world to see how happy I am and for them to know you're the reason." I gave her a peck on the lips.

"Really?"

"Really, really. Now let's go. We have a car coming for us in less than two hours." I couldn't believe she had agreed.

"Then let me up." She giggled, and I released her.

We got off the bed and ran toward the bathroom.

"All right. We'll shower together, but no sex," I warned.

"Yes, ma'am. But I'll get sex after the party, yeah?"

"If you're lucky, maybe even during." I nipped at her while the water heated up.

"Don't tease me." She sounded serious, but I knew she enjoyed it.

As I wrapped my arms around her, I held her close. "I love you."

"I love you more."

No way that was possible, but I wouldn't argue now. We were on a time crunch.

With five minutes to spare, we were dressed and ready to go. Jade looked like a rockstar. Her hair was slicked back and tucked behind her ears. She wore a black sleeveless jumpsuit resembling a tuxedo with lapels. But it was so sexy as it V-ed down to the waist, exposing the swell of her perky breasts. The legs were straight and pleated but capri length. It would be nice in this June heat.

With my black-and-gold dress, we coordinated perfectly. My outfit differed from what I'd imagined, but it was better. She changed it by V-ing the front and the back while leaving the sides open and held together by giant gold safety pins. There was a long, opened train with a layer of sparkly gold sheathing beneath it. It was sexy and sleek, and eye-catching. Together, we would turn heads.

When the car arrived, we climbed in, and the driver didn't say a word. As we rode in silence, I squeezed her thigh, and she wrapped her hand around mine.

"Are you sure you're ready? I can always have the driver take me back home." She leaned into me as she whispered, and her breath sent little shivers down my body.

"I'm one hundred percent sure. You belong with me."

She kissed me right below my ear, and I knew I didn't want to hide her or us. When I started living to make myself happy, it seemed everything else fell into place. Yeah, I didn't have my dream job, and my parents had written me off, but this was the most peaceful I'd ever been.

There wasn't a constant worry hanging over my head about other people's judgments. I could be myself and enjoy knowing I was loved for me. That was a feeling I'd never had before Jade, and it was something I wouldn't trade anything for. She was my chosen family, which was more than enough for me.

When we stopped, the driver told us we had arrived.

I let go of Jade's hand and opened the car door. As soon as I stepped out, there were camera crews and people everywhere. The sidewalk leading to the mansion was covered with red carpet as if it were a premiere event. The flashes went off, and I turned to see Jade emerging from the car. She scanned my body in her creation and appeared almost in awe.

When she finally locked eyes with me, I pulled her to my side. I laced our fingers together because I didn't want anyone to question that she was mine.

People yelled at me, but I ignored them as I reveled in this moment. This was me, showing everyone a part of myself that had been hidden for so long. I glanced at Jade, and she rubbed her thumb over my hand and then mouthed, "I love you." And I knew there was no one I'd rather have by my side, and she made me feel like I could conquer anything.

A few short weeks ago, I was lost. But I was a different person when I was with Jade. She gave me the courage to find myself, which led me to happiness. Before her, I was closed off to everyone, living a counterfeit life, trying to convince myself that being alone was my destiny. But now

I knew my life had felt empty because I'd surrounded myself with the wrong people.

The lights kept flashing, but all of my attention was on Jade. She was the most beautiful person in the room, and I couldn't have been prouder to have her on my arm. When we finally got to the entrance, Joanna was standing there with a cameraperson and her microphone out.

"Monica. Monica! Care to comment on your *date*?" she called out, and we stopped.

Jade gave her the stink eye, but I smiled graciously and pulled the mic from her hand.

"I do. This is Jade Miller, and she designed and made both of our amazing outfits tonight. Be on the lookout for her new boutique. Also, everyone better keep their hands off because she's mine."

I dropped the mic as I turned to Jade and cupped her face. She studied me as if trying to figure out what I was going to do, and without a moment's hesitation, I crashed my lips into hers, and she wrapped her arms around my waist, holding me tightly.

I could hear Joanna speaking, but I couldn't make it out as I blocked everything and got lost in my happily ever after.

Epilogue – Jade
THREE MONTHS LATER

"**A**re you excited about your big day?" I played with the hem of her shirt and brought her closer to me.

"Excited? I'm nervous as hell. What if I completely bomb out there?" Monica had landed the regional job at Gulf Side News, and she'd been on edge since finding out.

I gave her my what-the-fuck look. "That won't happen. You'll do great, and it will be the highest-rated show yet."

"But I haven't been on air in three months. I could have lost my mojo." She stared at me pleadingly, and I kissed her cheek.

"You most certainly didn't lose your mojo. At least you still had it as of this morning." I waggled my eyebrows, and she hit my arm.

"Stop it. You're not making it any better."

"All right. Tell me what I can do to help. I know you're going to do great. But how can I make you believe that?" I rested my forehead against hers.

She sighed. "How are you so sure?"

"Because I'm always right."

"So you think." She pulled her head back and rolled her eyes.

"Do I *think*, or do I *know*?"

She tried to push me away, but I held her tighter.

"Don't pretend like you disagree. I can't help that I know things."

"You're insufferable," she said while collapsing into my chest.

"Maybe, but at least I'm good in bed." I laughed as her coconut shampoo filled my nose, and it felt like home.

Since the Gala, a lot had changed for us. After Monica's plug on Channel 13, people took notice of my designs, and Monica thought it was prudent to strike while the iron was hot. So she sold her condo and moved into my place to help me get my boutique up and running.

Her faith in me was unwavering, and there was no way I could have accomplished this so soon. She didn't hesitate to invest her money in me, even though I fought her tooth and nail not to. But in the end, we were the proud owners of Mystique Designs, and she was my not-so-silent partner, which worked for us. I developed the ideas, and she made them better.

She shook her head as if exasperated by my comment. "I don't think we'll be testing that theory any time soon."

"Oh, babe. We both know it's not a theory—it's a fact." I beamed, and she playfully scoffed. "Are you feeling better?"

"Actually, I think I am."

I rubbed soothing circles on her back. "I know how to relax you down."

"That's not it. You annoyed me until I forgot what was bothering me." Her expression was serious, but I knew she was faking.

"You say tomato. I say ketchup."

"What?" She pulled out of my arms, laughing.

"See, I was right. I can always loosen you up." I leaned in, kissing her. "I love you."

"I love you, too." Her cobalt eyes softened, and I knew I would never look at anyone like I did her. "Drive me to the studio?"

"Of course. The more time I have with you, the better. Now, get ready." I smacked her bottom, and she gave me a warning glare.

Two hours later, we were in her dressing room at Gulf Side Station.

"Wow. This is a proper dressing room. It's huge." I spun around before plopping down on the full-sized plush couch. "And look at the wardrobe. Where's your stylist?" I was in awe of how big-time she was.

"We're early, so they might not be here for a while."

"Oh yeah? Early enough for..." I patted the seat next to me, and she appeared shocked.

"My God. We are not doing that on my first day. I'd prefer not to get fired."

"Doing what? I thought we would talk more about your concerns." I flashed my best smile, and she saw right through it.

"You only have one thing on your mind, and it's not talking."

I rubbed my chin like I was stroking a beard. "Hmm. I'm starting to believe it's you who has a one-track mind, and you're projecting your desires onto me."

"Right, Freud. Try to—"

A knock interrupted her thought, and she went to answer the door. "Oh my God! Scott! What are you doing here?"

"Ms. Starr. It's good to see you." He beamed at her. "I'm on staff and didn't tell you because I thought it would be a nice surprise."

She stared at him. "I can't believe you could keep a secret from me."

"It was hard not telling you, but the look on your face was worth it."

She practically jumped into his arms, and I was glad he was here. Having another familiar face in the crowd would help make her feel more confident.

"I'm just so happy to see you!"

"Me too." He set her down and looked at me. "Jade. How's it going? Staying out of trouble?" He asked me that every time he saw me now, even though punching Joanna was the only act of violence I'd ever committed or ever would again.

"Sir, yes, sir. I'm reformed. That detainment scared me straight." Not really, but I saw the error of my ways, and violence was never the answer, no matter how much someone pissed me off.

"Good to know. How is work going?" He came over, joining me on the couch.

"Very well. A department store is submitting an offer on some of my designs, and I'm hopeful the contract will be acceptable to the missus." I nodded toward Monica.

"Don't act like I'm the boss. I just don't want you to lose creative control, so I would prefer to look everything over before blindly agreeing." She narrowed her eyes, and I gave Scott a "see what I mean" look, and he laughed.

"Whatever. I'm watching out for you." Her gaze was getting icy, and I decided to give it a break.

"I'm teasing. You know how much I appreciate you. We both know I wouldn't be here without your support and assertiveness." I blew her a kiss.

"That's a fancy way of saying I'm bossy."

I glanced at Scott, who was biting his lip to keep from smiling.

"What?" I shook my head. "I've never thought you were bossy. Did you?" I turned to Scott, and he held his hands up in surrender.

She sat down in her chair and faced away from us. "You two think you're so funny. Well, you can laugh out in the hallway. I have to get ready." She waved her hand toward the door.

Scott and I stared at each other. Then I glanced at Monica, who locked eyes with me in the mirror. Memories of us at the old studio came flooding back, and I felt heat creeping up my neck. She must have had the same thought as a knowing smile crossed her face. Every day I fell a little harder for her because she continued to show me more.

Life had a funny way of working out, and most of the time, it was unexpected. If I had told my eighteen-year-old self that this was how I would end up, she would have laughed in my face. I could still remember sitting in Spanish class, drawing her, hoping one day she would see me the way I saw her.

Now, even though she was all but kicking me out of her dressing room, I knew she was mine, and we belonged to each other. It made me wonder if all my wishing turned my dreams into a reality.

I walked over and kissed her cheek before whispering, "Good luck, and I love you." Then I said to Scott, "It looks like we've been dismissed."

"Oh. It wouldn't be the first time," he boomed.

"Out!" She smiled and mouthed, "I love you too."

We had a long history, and it was interesting how two opposites fit perfectly together. We had our share of disappointments in this world, but we didn't let them keep us down. And now we were stronger and more compassionate because of our experiences.

Even though our journeys were different, I was grateful that our paths finally aligned because we brought out the best in each other.

Also by Abigail Taylor

THE UNDERDOG SERIES

Falling Blindly (Book 1)

Chasing Life (Book 2)

Seeking Redemption (Book 3)

FRIENDS AND LOVERS SERIES

No One Compares to Her (Book 1)

She Keeps Me Warm (Book 2)

I Need Her Love (Book 3)

SPECIAL OCCASIONS SERIES

My Gift to You (Book 1)

Unwrap Me (Book 2)

STANDALONE

She's Home

FREE STORY

A New Direction - A Friends and Lovers Series Prequel

POETRY

Destruction to Devotion

See Me Now

Acknowledgments

I want to thank you so much for following Jade and Monica's story. I hope you enjoyed their journey, and I truly appreciate your continued support.

I also want to thank my fantastic team who have kept me going during these last few difficult months. They have pushed me to continue following my dreams, which was something I didn't know if I could do.

About the Author

Abigail Taylor is a contemporary LGBTQ+ romance author and self-confessed music junkie. She's a workout enthusiast who has completed several Tough Mudders where she swam in ice baths and was even electrocuted.

She loves doing things outside of her comfort zone and pushing boundaries, but when it comes to romance, she loves a happy ending!

Abigail enjoys traveling the world, meeting new people, and trying new experiences such as jumping from a plane at 9,000 feet, but for now, she's busy giving life to her characters.

Thank you for all of your support!

You can keep in contact with me through:

- Email (abbytaylorauthor@gmail.com)
- Instagram (@abbytaylorauthor)
- Twitter (twitter.com/a_taylorauthor)
- Facebook (facebook.com/abigailtaylorauthor)
- Amazon (amazon.com/author/abigailtaylor)
- Website (abbytaylorauthor.com)

Printed in Great Britain
by Amazon

38808793R00106